Yashodhara

A Novel

VOLGA

Translated from the Telugu by P.S.V. Prasad

HARPER**PERENNIAL**

An Imprint of HarperCollins Publishers

First published in India in 2019 by Harper Perennial An
Imprint of HarperCollins *Publishers*
Building No 10, Tower A, 4th Floor, DLF Cyber City, Phase II,
Gurugram – 122002
www.harpercollins.co.in

1 2 3 4 5 6 7 8 9 10

Copyright © Volga 2019
Originally published as *Yashobuddha* in 2017 by
Swechcha Publishers
English Translation Copyright © P.S.V. Prasad 2019

P-ISBN: 978-93-5302-589-2
E-ISBN: 978-93-5302-590-8

This is a work of fiction and all characters and incidents described in this book are the product of the author's imagination. Any resemblance to actual persons, living or dead, is entirely coincidental.

Volga asserts the moral right
to be identified as the author of this work

All rights reserved. No part of this publication may be reproduced, stored in a retrieval system, or transmitted, in any form or by any means, electronic, mechanical, photocopying, recording or otherwise, without the prior permission of the publishers.

Typeset in 11.5/16 Joanna MT Std at
Manipal Digital Systems, Manipal

Yashodhara

Volga is one of the most significant figures in contemporary Telugu literature. Her nearly-fifty publications include novels, plays, short-story collections, collections of essays and poetry, as well as translations. Presently the executive chairperson and founder member of *Asmita Resource Centre for Women*, Volga has edited the anthology of poems *Neeli Meghalu*, co-edited *Sarihaddulu Leni Sandhyalu*, which deals with feminist political praxis in Andhra Pradesh and co-authored the book *Saramsam*, which documents the anti-arrack struggle. She has co-authored *Mahilavaranam/Womanscape*, a volume on celebrating the women who shaped the history of Andhra Pradesh.

Volga has received several awards for her work, including the Best Writer Award from Potti Sriramulu Telugu University, the Rangavalli Memorial Award, the Ramineni Foundation Award, the Malathi Chandur Award, the Visala Sahiti Puraskaram, the Suseela Narayana Reddy Award, the Kandukuri Veerasalingam Literary Award, the Loknayak Foundation Award, the South Asia Laadli Media & Advertising Award for Gender Sensitivity. She received the Sahitya Akademi Award in 2015 for her novel *Vimuktha*, published in English as *The Liberation of Sita* by Harper Perennial.

P.S.V. Prasad worked as associate professor in the department of English in Chundi Ranganayakulu Degree College and retired as its principal in 2013. He is the author of the the Telugu novel *Samathavani* and has written the scripts for two Telugu films, *Mamasri* and *Aswani*, for which he received the Kalasagar best film writer award.

To Thich Nhat Hanh
for his poetry, full of compassion towards life

It was the twilight of an evening. The light of the sun, setting behind the hills, was slowly altering its colour. White clouds reflected it in one hue while the black in another. Yashodhara went into a trance as she looked at the wonderful variations of dark purple and crimson that stretched across the vast cloudy expanse. She didn't even notice that the trees around her were slowly being covered by a sheet of darkness. It was her habit to be at that garden every evening, gather flowers, offer some to the deity in the nearby temple and take home the remaining. That day, she was a little late as there were guests at home and she had to help her mother in discharging the duties of hospitality. But so what if she were late! It offered her the good fortune of witnessing the most beautiful sunset behind the hills that were visible through the gaps between the line of trees where she stood.

Though the sun had now set behind the hills and was resting, his rays were still painting the sky in multiple shades of red. At last, Yashodhara brought down her gaze from the unreachable colours in the sky to the colourful flowers that were within her hand's reach. Gathering flowers was the work that pleased her most. She would take only a few chosen flowers from each tree and, for doing that, she would go on apologizing each of them. She engaged herself in an unending dialogue with the trees. She said she was sorry for severing them from their children and promised that she would use them to adorn the goddess in the temple.

With the flowers she had collected, Yashodhara stepped into the courtyard of the temple. The next moment, she was transfixed to the spot. Her feet refused to step forward any farther. For, there, on a stone slab to the left of the courtyard, she beheld a youth of incredible distinction. Just as the magnificent sunset had allured her eyes, the sight of the stranger, like the beautiful moonrise, filled her heart with inexplicable ecstasy. He seemed young. His serene and radiant face was without a trace of pride that often accompanied youth. It diffused only light – light that got neither scattered nor altered. No one could tell what his mind seemed to be occupied with, but it was certain that whatever it was, it was full of peace and wonder for there played the steadiest and most tender smile upon his lips. The way he sat – with his palms folded on his lap and his feet in the padmasana posture – Yashodhara's eyes were transfixed. Gradually, she came back to her senses. Gathering her wits with difficulty, but with a decisive mind, she went into the temple. She offered flowers and her obeisance to the goddess and stepped out of the sanctum. As she walked along the corridor, she looked at him again and without meaning to, she let out a deep sigh. Then, she hurried past the garden to reach her home, anxious about how late she was.

However, it was only her body that reached home. In spite of its mechanical responses, her mind was elsewhere. She could hear her parents and answer their questions, she could see people at work around her, but it seemed like there was a haze between herself and the world. She filled her stomach with food, unaware of the actual tastes. Her bed, to which she was habituated, invited her to lie down and sleep in order to overcome her weariness. But sleep, whether she was angry with or afraid of Yashodhara, pledged herself not to be in her vicinity. Her eyelids remained separated, as if they could not bear the touch of each other, and her eyes played a trick on her: bringing up the image of the young man and the calmness he emanated as he sat meditating.

That night, when Siddhartha Gautama was at dinner, Mahaprajapati Gotami, his mother, sat by his side, trying to serve him a little more and then some more of his favourite dishes. On his part, Siddhartha Gautama tried his best to prevent her. Both, in turns, succeeded in getting the upper hand. After their meal, the mother and the son would sit in the garden, engaging themselves in song and music. That evening, Siddhartha was in a hurry to finish his meal as he longed to fill his heart with music. It was a peaceful, moonlit night. Stars faded and failed to twinkle, even as bright moonlight flooded the sky. But here on the earth, the mother and the son were twinkling like jewels. There was a pond in front of their seat and it was surrounded by trees in full bloom, with fragrant flowers that spread their distinct scents all around. Here and there, there were lights which shone like stars that had descended to the earth.

Siddhartha was unaware of himself and his surroundings as he sang in full-throated ease. Enraptured by the melody of his voice, the moon looked as if it would melt and flow down to the earth. Gotami joined her voice in tune with him.

When Siddhartha stopped singing, he looked around in admiration and said, 'Mother! Doesn't the whole universe seem to be dancing in one rhythmic step?'

Gotami nodded her head in agreement. She loved to hear Siddhartha speak. Whatever his thoughts were, he transformed them into words that conveyed to his listeners a new meaning – a meaning that made them see a new truth. Familiar words, when uttered by Siddhartha, sounded so new that one wondered whether anyone had spoken them before.

Gotami received the message that Suddhodana wanted to speak to her. When his mother had left, Siddhartha tried to relax himself in the moonlight, lying on the hard ground beside the pond. Steadily staring at the bright moon, he lay there awake for a long time. His eyes worshipped the beauty of nature until they were satiated, and then they slowly closed themselves to rest.

Siddhartha loved to open his eyes to the light of daybreak but he disliked the daytime as he had to do many things which always displeased him. He had to lend a patient ear to his father, who would explain at length the details of agricultural income and expenditure. He had to spend long hours learning the skills of a warrior – sword fighting, wrestling, archery and many more. After his midday meal, he would rest for a while and only afterwards, in the evening, he would find time to visit the Sramanas he liked most. His feet would lead him in a hurry to the ashram of the ascetics to meet Kalamuni, the one he was closest to. There his intellect would be awakened.

With the help of Kalamuni, he would seek answers to questions that puzzled his mind and tormented his heart. His discussions with Kalamuni widened his thought processes and deepened his wisdom. He would shoot out an endless array of questions – questions about creation, about nature, about energy, about emotions and experiences, and about the joys and sorrows of human life. That was the time most valuable to him. The intensity of their daily discussions would make him highly emotional and restless. His heart, ablaze with unrest and anguish, would beat rapidly. In order to regain his equilibrium, he would go and sit in meditation at the temple near Kalamuni's ashram. Doubt and disturbance that marked his countenance would gradually be replaced by profuse light and peace. Blessed would be the people who beheld that spectacle. He looked as if he were the embodiment of all human virtues put together in one human form. At that moment, it would be impossible to compare him with others – even with a saint or with a god. He was unique. He was just Siddhartha and that was all.

That afternoon Siddhartha did not want to rest and so time seemed to be moving at a slow pace. In the evening, he prepared to go out earlier than the usual time. On his way to Kalamuni's ashram, he came across a group of Sramanas, and he stood staring at them till they were out of his sight. The question why they chose to lead the life of ascetics perplexed him. In spite of being rich, did they renounce all material pleasures to live a simple life? Or, unable to bear the hard realities of life, were they trying to run away from them? Such questions baffled him whenever he saw them. His own life was not devoid of sorrow. There was a tragedy in it, a severe loss that could never be compensated. It resulted in suffering that could not be quenched with tears. The pain it caused was too difficult to bear, but he had to bear it all when he was only ten years old.

Till he was ten, Siddhartha was of the opinion that Mahaprajapati Gotami was his mother. But one day Devadatta, enraged by his defeat at sport, called him a 'motherless fellow'. When Siddhartha demanded an explanation, he simply said that Gotami was Siddhartha's stepmother and his mother was Mahamaya who died a few days after his birth. Saying so, Devadatta ran away. At that time, Siddhartha could not clearly understand what the word 'stepmother' meant. But, somehow, it opened within him a deep pain – a pain he had never experienced before in his life. Whenever he was wounded at play and was bleeding, he took it sportively and laughed. Long hours of training in archery tired his body, but not his mind. Little cuts he received during his sword-fighting training sessions never pained him. But now this pain caused by the word motherless was very different – it was strangely new to him. At once he went to Gotami, told her about his pain and begged her to reveal the truth about the matter.

Gotami told him everything – the truth about his birth. She told him how Mahamaya Devi took him into her womb as a seed, gave him life, fed him, shaped and sheltered him for ten months before bringing him into the world. She described in detail all about Mahamaya Devi – her physical charm, her dignified demeanour, her love of nature and her adoration for beauty. It was her deep longing for beauty that drew her to the gardens near Lumbini when she was near the end of her pregnancy. There, while walking through the beautiful flower garden, she gave birth to Siddhartha – a blend of the qualities of the sun and the moon. Mahamaya Devi could hold him close to her heart only for seven days. Then the bond between the mother and the son got severed abruptly. Siddhartha listened to it all with attention, When Gotami narrated how, after the death of Mahamaya, she had taken him onto her lap and become his mother, Siddhartha hugged her. For several nights after that, Siddhartha wept and grieved for his mother whom he had never seen, and he experienced great pain.

There was another thought that constantly festered in his mind. Was he the cause for his mother's sudden death?

His father, Suddhodana, tried his best to appease him. Gotami felt tired of telling him again and again that all women at the time of childbirth almost reach death and return; and that Mahamaya Devi also returned from thence. She made it clear to him that he was not responsible for her illness caused after his birth. It was at that time that Suddhodana made Siddhartha visit a saint – a man of great wisdom. The saint firmly explained that one must bear one's own responsibility for one's own death. His words eased the intensity of pain in Siddhartha's heart. But he was not totally set free from the questions about death. He was able to accept the truth that his mother had died, but he wanted to know if there was any eternal truth about death. If there really was one, what was it? The questions that sprouted in his mind took root deep within him and started growing along with him. He knew his mother would never return. He knew she was no longer in existence. He knew he would have to bear that painful truth throughout his life. But the way he understood it now was different from the way he understood it then. His attitude had changed over the years. The abyss between 'to be in existence' and 'not to be in existence', he was able to perceive now, not only in relation to his mother but in relation to all things around him. The joys and sorrows behind them were just experiences. He was trying to locate the seat of experience, but it seemed to elude his comprehension. His discussions with Kalamuni brought him new cognizance about many things. But at the same time, new questions arose out of the new knowledge, and he needed answers to them. Were the Sramanas able to find answers? Or were they eternally in search of them?

Engrossed in deep thought, Siddhartha forgot all about going to Kalamuni's ashram, and after a long, insentient wandering, he reached home.

That evening Siddhartha did not feel like eating and did not even want to engage in music. But, if he said so, his parents would be greatly disturbed. The whole household would be worried. Instead of plunging them in sorrow, he thought it would be better for him to overcome his restlessness by being in the presence of Gotami – eating and singing as he always did. That night, he could not sleep. He was disturbed by the thoughts of his mother. His inability to forget Mahamaya Devi might mean that he was disowning and dishonouring Mahaprajapati Gotami. Just because he was not born of her womb, should he doubt her love and affection for him? No, it wasn't that. It wasn't that at all.

His heart longed to feel the touch, the gentle caress of the mother who had given him birth. That was all.

There was a little emptiness in his mind – an emptiness to be filled with the image of his mother. People who knew Mahamaya Devi considered him to be her replica. But, sadly, the original image had vanished while the duplicate survived. Who named her Mahamaya? *The supreme illusion!* Was the whole universe delivered into existence by a supreme Mahamaya? What was the truth behind that illusion? He was left in the world by Mahamaya to experience sorrow, separation and a longing that could never be satisfied. If all such feelings were illusion; what would be the absolute truth? Would it be possible to behold it? In what way?

His thoughts stretched beyond night, into daybreak, to fill his eyes with the redness of dawn. He stood at the window, facing the sun for a while and then went away to commence his routine work.

Suddhodana was engaged in a discussion with the elders of different villages surrounding Kapilavastu. They were all comfortably seated in the big hall. When Siddhartha entered the hall, he found the elders in profound silence and felt greatly relieved. At such meetings, the elders would generally be found engaged in heated arguments and bitter quarrels, hardly ever in such eerie silence. That was why, whenever his father sent for him, Siddhartha would at first try to find an excuse to avoid going there. But his inability to tell lies would finally compel him to attend the discussions. On that day too, he went there reluctantly. But, to his great surprise, he found the elders silent.

It was the time when the fields had to be irrigated. It was also the time when, in general, Kapilavastu would be engaged in bitter disputes and sometimes in feuds with neighbouring kingdoms over the distribution of the waters of the Rohini River. The elders sitting so silently at such a critical time was the cause of Siddhartha's surprise. He walked slowly to his seat and sat down. 'Father! Why are you all so silent today?' he said looking at Suddhodana.

'Nothing special, Siddhartha. The Rohini is in full flow this year. No need to contend with our neighbours for our share of her waters. We feel that it is not necessary for us to prepare for war this year.'

Siddhartha's face lit up. 'Your decision is just,' he said. 'It is good to have plenty of water. But, father, I have another thought. In order to enjoy peace, we need plenty. It may be water, it may be food or it may include any other kind of wealth.'

Almost always, most people failed to understand whatever Siddhartha said. Some understood only the husks of the words. But those who grasped the inner meaning felt greatly pleased by his prudence.

One of the elders, Devamsa, said, 'Abundance does not depend on human effort alone, Siddhartha. As there has been sufficient rainfall this year, there is plenty of water for irrigation. But, does this happen every year? Just as the rainfall is not in our control, peace too is not entirely in our hands. You think too much about peace. But you must understand that our repeated requests for peace will be viewed as our weakness at warfare. Whether the Rohini is flooding its banks or flowing merely as a trickle, we should always better ourselves at warfare.'

Siddhartha was annoyed with what Devamsa said. It took him a little while to regain his composure. Suddhodana could clearly read the expression of disappointment on Siddhartha's face. He pitied his son.

'You are still young, Siddhartha,' he would tell his son on such occasions. 'You are asked to attend these meetings so that you will acquire worldly knowledge. Your duty is to listen carefully and understand. You can express your opinions when you are a little more grown up.'

Siddhartha, on his part, would sincerely try to follow his father's advice. But, when he heard words that incited war, he would forget everything else. Words that stressed the importance of peace would, then, automatically flow out of his mouth. His ideas about peace would make the warmongers grind their teeth and they would enter into an argument with him, even though to them he was only a boy. Yet, very soon they would understand that it would be impossible for them to contradict his ideas. Embittered by their helplessness, they would leave the place in a fit of fury.

Devamsa's remarks about war and peace excited Siddhartha and drew him into an argument. 'Oh noble lord!' he said, joining his palms in salutation to Devamsa. 'If we can peacefully share the waters of the Rohini when she is in plenty; we can also peacefully share when she is in scarce. We are all like the twin sons of mother earth. One should not be suckled at the expense of the other. If human beings learn to share not simply her riches, but also her poverty, they will have no cause for war and for grief. Only peace will prevail on the face of Mother Earth.'

Devamsa felt angry. He did not like to be taught the meanings of words by a youngster who was hardly twenty years of age.

'Suddhodana!' he said sternly. 'I am not a fool to be guided by the advice of children and, with your permission, I shall take leave of you all.'

As Devamsa walked out of the assembly, the other elders stood up, noisily talking against Siddhartha. Suddhodana joined his palms in reverence to the elders and declared that the assembly was over. He humbly asked them to forgive him if they were put to any inconvenience at his home.

Siddhartha walked out of the gathering nonchalantly. He pitied the elders who desired war in place of peace. These elders would always decide in favour of war. It would result in the loss of life of innocent people. And there wasn't any assurance that another war wouldn't break out before the wails of the kith and kin of the dead subsided.

Having left his house, Siddhartha started walking through agricultural fields. The full-grown, green crops in the fields, enjoying the warmth of the sun, swayed their heads invitingly. Suddenly, a lamb came running from somewhere and stood in front of him, tempting him to take her into his arms. Siddhartha squatted on the ground and took the lamb onto his lap. As the lamb lifted her head and looked lovingly at him, he was set free from all the unrest in his heart. Could there be a more wonderful scene to watch than the scene of Siddhartha amid green fields, sharing love and affection with a white lamb on his lap!

Just then, Yashodhara, along with the daughters of her uncle, happened to pass along that way. She was trying to discipline the two mischievous girls when she was arrested by the sight of Siddhartha. At that point, something amused the two girls and they burst into wild laughter. Siddhartha turned his head and looked at them. The girls were lured by the white lamb. They ran to it and tried to take it into their arms. The lamb slipped out of their hands and ran away. The girls ran after it.

Yashodhara and Siddhartha stood facing each other. Neither of the two dared to move from their spots. In a little while the two girls returned and, with helplessness written all over their faces, complained that the lamb was lost. Yashodhara held their hands and started walking along the path they had come. She did not know why she had done so. She was disturbed and confused by Siddhartha's presence there.

After she had left, Siddhartha stood at the spot for a long time. The heat of the sun burnt his skin, but he did not feel it. He was benumbed, devoid of sensation and thought. Even when he was in deep meditation, he would understand when his thoughts strolled astray; and with little effort, he would guide them aright. But it was different today. His mind was incapable of thinking. It simply didn't exist. His mind and body seemed to have disappeared from this physical world. Was it a new experience? Or, was it his inexperience?

A farmer on his way to his fields saw Siddhartha and patted him on his shoulder. 'Young man!' he said. 'What makes you stand here in the hot sun?' Siddhartha looked confusedly at the farmer.

'Look, how your face has tanned! You are getting drenched in sweat. Go home, young man. Are you thirsty? Shall I give you a drink of water?'

Siddhartha nodded his head, drank a mouthful of water, turned back and plodded in the direction of Kapilavastu.

———

Yashodhara was the daughter of Bimbanana, a landlord of Koliya village, which lay adjacent to Kapilavastu. Bimbanana was more interested in the Vedas than in agriculture. As he belonged to the Kshatriya caste, he was often found performing religious rituals like the yagnas and the yagas. He honoured Brahmin pundits and invited them to his home for philosophical discussions.

Yashodhara would sit beside her father during such discussions. Though she understood little of what was being discussed, she would lend a patient ear to the renowned scholars of the day.

Once, when she was a little older, and was able to understand the ways of the world, Yashodhara witnessed an animal being sacrificed at the end of a yagna. She was horrified. She felt dizzy and fell down unconscious. Bimbanana was angry with his wife, Visista, for allowing Yashodhara to attend the ritual of animal sacrifice. From that day, Yashodhara gave up eating meat. A strong aversion for yagnas and yagas developed in her heart. She began hating the Brahmin priests who extolled the importance of religious rituals and encouraged her father to perform them. She felt that all the religious practices they were teaching were aimed at safeguarding their own communal interests in society. Once or twice, she tried to argue with her father, but he was reluctant to discuss such matters with her. He gently scolded her, saying that women were not qualified to talk about religion and philosophy. Yashodhara felt deeply hurt by her father's rebuke. The idea that women were incapable of nobler thoughts pained her sensitive heart.

As the only child of her parents, Yashodhara was brought up with utmost love and affection. When she grew older, she was able to understand that her social freedom and movements were limited because she was a girl. Time and again, her mother would tell her how she should conduct herself at her husband's home and how her good conduct would make her parents feel proud of her. Yashodhara never felt pleased with her mother's advice. The thought of marriage, a husband and his parents, always made her anxious. She sincerely prayed to the goddess at home and the goddess in the temple to shape her life such that she could live forever with her parents, in the house where she was born. However, as she grew older, she gradually realized that perhaps even the goddess was helpless in that regard.

That evening, when Yashodhara had first set her eyes upon Siddhartha, her head was troubled with anxious thoughts of her marriage. She was unable to forget his serene face. The second time when she saw him in the fields, she strongly felt that she had to marry him. Now she was no more worried about her marriage. No other thought entered her mind except the thought of her marriage with him. Would it be possible for her to marry him? That question never entered her mind. She did not know any of his personal details; his name, parentage or place of residence. Yet, she firmly decided that she should have him – no one but him – as her husband.

However, she could not share her thoughts with others. She felt that she could not ask anyone about him just yet. It did not seem necessary for her to know his details. For a few days, she spent all her time thinking about him and enjoying the pleasure derived out of it.

Yashodhara was greatly disturbed when she heard that her father, Bimbanana, was in search of a suitable husband for her. She felt that she must do something before it was too late. There was a chance for her to meet Siddhartha at the temple. But strangely she did not find him there again though she had been regularly going to the temple. She spent hours trying to find a plausible reason for his absence and finally hit upon the fact that she must have been late in going to the temple on that day when she had seen him for the first time. That fact relieved her of anxiety. The rest of the day she spent joyfully doing some work or other. She helped her mother unasked. The next evening, she did not get ready to go to the temple at the usual time. Her mother was surprised.

'Won't you bring flowers this evening? Shall I send someone else?' she asked, looking a little concerned.

At that, Yashodhara picked up the flower basket and left her house for the temple.

The temple was on the outskirts of both Koliya and Kapilavastu villages, but nearer to Koliya than to Kapilavastu. As it took much time to get there, most people avoided it. Only those who had an eye for the beauty of nature occasionally visited it; and such people knew well that Siddhartha regularly went there to sit in meditation for some time. They carefully avoided walking near him lest he be disturbed.

Yashodhara was not in a hurry to reach the temple. But at last, when she got there, she did not find Siddhartha, and she was disappointed. She spent some time slowly filling her basket with flowers, but still there was no sign of his arrival. She went into the temple and sat in front of the stone slab where she had seen Siddhartha meditating. But after a short while she realized her mistake. Wouldn't Siddhartha turn back and go away if he found someone right in front of the place where he meditated? The thought frightened her. She left the place at once and hid herself behind a pillar which was just beside the stone slab. There, she would not be visible to people when they stepped into the temple.

With the passage of time, tension was mounting up in Yashodhara every second. She waited and waited till her heart skipped a beat and her eyes glowed with joy. For there, at the entrance, she beheld Siddhartha walking in majestically.

Siddhartha entered the courtyard of the temple, went to the stone slab and sat down in the padmasana posture. When he was about to close his eyes, he suddenly sensed something unusual in the environment that he knew so well. He felt that he was being watched by someone very close to him. He turned his head aside to see who the person was. The next moment his eyes widened.

Yashodhara did not wish to waste her time. 'May I know your name?' she said.

'Siddhartha Gautama.'

The words just slipped out of his mouth. He did not know who she was and why she wanted to make acquaintance with him. He did not wish to know anything about her before revealing his identity.

'Who are your parents? Your dynasty!'

'Suddhodana is my father. Mahaprajapati Gotami, my mother. We are of the Sakya dynasty.'

That was all Yashodhara wanted to know. She stood up to go. Siddhartha also raised himself up. He wanted to ask who she was, but he couldn't.

Yashodhara, who walked forward a few steps, stopped, turned back and went up to him. She held his hand, took a handful of flowers from the basket and put them in his wide, cupped palms.

'I am Yashodhara, daughter of Bimbanana and Visista of the Koliya dynasty,' she said. Then she looked at him, smiled and hurried away.

It took Siddhartha quite some time to come back to his senses. He looked at the flowers in his hand and carefully bundled them with his shawl. Giving up his meditation for that evening, he left the place carrying the weightless bundle on his shoulder.

On her way home, all that Yashodhara thought about was Siddhartha. Now that she knew his name and address, she wanted to find out all about his character. He possessed a strong and elegant physique. His eyes, always filled with compassion, showed that he was sensitive at heart. But she wanted to be certain. Could she find a way to know it?

As soon as she reached home, she handed the basket of flowers to her mother and called her cousins to come and sit with her. She told them a story about lambs. The girls listened with rapt attention and soon they were reminded of the little lamb that had escaped from their arms. 'Wish we could hold that little lamb again,' one of the girls said and sighed.

Yashodhara smiled, knowing that her plan was working. 'Do you know to whom it belongs?' she asked them.

The girls shrugged their shoulders.

'It belongs to Siddhartha Gautama. Tell your father to get it from him. Didn't it look extraordinarily beautiful? I'm quite sure the lamb has magical powers. Otherwise, how could it disappear at a wink the other day? Don't you want to own such a wonderful lamb? Go; go and ask your father now!'

The girls could not resist their temptation for the white lamb. They set out at once in search of their father. Yashodhara followed them to her uncle's house.

The girls ran to their father, sat by his side and asked him to get them Siddhartha's white lamb. Their father smiled at them and sent them away with the promise that he would get the white lamb for them.

'What! Is Siddhartha Gautama rearing sheep?' said one of the elderly men, who was talking to him.

'Yes, he is sure to do such things. The other day, at the assembly of elders arranged by Suddhodana, he was saying that we should love all living beings, and that we should not resort to animal sacrifice during yagnas. Who knows! He may own all our animals; deprive us of animals for sacrifice,' another man said, laughing loudly through his thick, bushy moustache.

'I don't understand how a Kshatriya could be so delicate. If he hears the word "war", he will go on delivering a lecture about peace till we drop down our bows and arrows.'

'He doesn't seem to respect Vedic rites, and the people who perform them.'

'Now I understand why he rears sheep. A fellow who has given up the duties of a Kshatriya and the knowledge of the Vedas — what better work does he find than rearing sheep!'

Everyone laughed loudly.

Yashodhara also laughed. She laughed to the satisfaction of her heart.

Siddhartha was always attentive, never inattentive. He did the right work at the right time and did it with much concentration. He seemed to have acquired punctuality and sincerity naturally by birth. In everything he did, from the simplest to the most difficult, he showed great devotion. People who watched him at work always admired and applauded his undivided attention. When it came to meditation, his concentration was at its highest. He could effortlessly sit down and meditate even when people were moving around him.

That night, at supper, Gotami could understand that Siddhartha was not at all attentive. She was stunned when she saw him swallowing his food without looking at what he was eating.

'Siddhartha!' she said with much concern, 'I have never seen you so inattentive before. What's the matter with you, my son? Are you all right?'

It was not in Siddhartha's nature to hide his thoughts and feelings, and put forward false pretexts. Whatever was on his mind, he would honestly share with others. He looked at her and smiled.

'Mother!' he said softly, almost in a whisper. 'My meditation, this evening, was interrupted by someone – a stranger.'

'Why should anyone disturb you?' Gotami said, looking a little worried.

'I do not know who she is, Mother. I saw her once in the fields a few days ago. This evening, when I was settling down for meditation at the temple, she came up to me and asked me for my name and my family name. She said she was Yashodhara, the daughter of Bimbanana and Visista of Koliya village. While going away, she stopped and returned to me. She put a handful of flowers in my hand and then went away. All this seems to me so wonderful and so joyous. But, at the same time, it alarms me much, and I feel heavy at heart. Mother! I have never come across such a feeling in my life till now.'

As she listened carefully to each word of Siddhartha, Gotami's face appeared brighter and brighter. Her eyes were filled with tears of joy.

'Do not be worried, Siddhartha,' she said, wiping her tears. 'Be happy, my dear,' she continued, 'it's all for your good. Whatever you have felt at the temple, and whatever you are feeling now is real and true. All that is true and real, you must accept.'

Gotami affectionately passed her hand over Siddhartha's head.

After Siddhartha had gone to bed, Gotami went to see Suddhodana, and she recounted what Siddhartha had told her.

'That girl seems to be very extraordinary,' remarked Suddhodana, after listening carefully to what she said. 'How dare she talk to a stranger that way! I know her father. He strictly adheres to the duties prescribed to the Kshatriyas. He honours the Brahmin scholars and performs yagnas and yagas.'

As he spoke, Gotami looked at him thoughtfully and smiled. 'Don't you consider her to be the most suitable bride for Siddhartha?' she said. 'No one has been able to distract our son from his meditation till now; and no girl has ever drawn his attention so heartily. You see, I think we shall be freed from all our anxieties if Siddhartha gets married to this girl.'

'You are right. All this while, we have been hesitating to talk to him about getting married. Now Siddhartha himself has given us that chance. Send for the girl's father tomorrow, without delay.'

The thought that Siddhartha would finally think of a marriage proposition made both of them extremely happy. For the last few years, they were constantly getting worried by Siddhartha's growing love for meditation, his friendship with the ascetics and his aversion to the duties prescribed to his caste. They knew that Siddhartha was not in favour of getting married, and so they avoided talking about it in his presence.

Suddhodana, at his wife's suggestion, felt that it would be better for him to meet Bimbanana and discuss the matter with him.

Meanwhile, Siddhartha was carefully analysing his experience with Yashodhara. He was aware of feelings such as love, pity, affection, kindness and friendship. They always dwelt in his heart. But his feeling for Yashodhara – it seemed to be above all such feelings. It was different – inexplicably wonderful. It filled his heart with a sweet pain which he had never experienced before. Feelings like love and compassion had always touched his heart and pleased his mind at the emotional level, but the new feeling touched his body as well, and pleased him both emotionally and sensually. It was, perhaps, the natural physical attraction that takes place between a woman and a man, he thought. His love for his mother and all other beings in the world was entirely different from his love for Yashodhara. What was so different between the two? He wanted to know. As always, he thought very deeply about it, and in a few minutes he was able to understand it. When he thought about his mother and everyone else he cared about, the dominant force in him was his desire to offer them his love. He did not want anything in return. But now, this young lady had kindled in his heart the desire to receive.

Never before in his life did Siddhartha yearn so strongly to receive anything. He was blessed with a life in which he was provided with everything he needed, unasked. It was, perhaps, for that reason that Siddhartha did not learn to yearn for material objects. All his attention was drawn towards the immaterial and the spiritual, and he valued them more. He spent much of his time thinking about the universe, its creation and its relation to human life. The Sramanas and the spiritual teachers, who led a different life from the ordinary people, attracted him. He respected them as they were involved in a profoundly spiritual quest. However, Yashodhara diverted his attention from the spiritual plane to the physical plane. This new, powerful feeling, like an ocean, engulfed him. Besides his eagerness to offer love, the desire to receive it sprouted in his heart, put forth tender leaves and shone brightly.

Yashodhara was set free from all her doubts and worries. She was buoyant with joy. She hardly had any empty space in her mind to fill it with dreams about the life she would lead with Siddhartha Gautama. It was all filled up with boundless love for him. To spend her time, till she met him again, was the greatest problem for her, now. As time was set in motion, she sat watching its movement around her. She watched the night pass away and she watched the dawn set in.

Everything pleased her eyes. She watched the warm sun and the cool breeze contrive together to make the flowers sway their heads and make them laugh with joy. The sun climbed up into the sky to make the world warm and energetic. Bubbling with energy, people started attending to their daily tasks. They talked and walked, laughed and worked, cooled their bodies with sweat, satisfied their hunger with food and pleased their minds with conversation. As if to sabotage their attempts, the sun shot out his millions and millions of innumerable rays. But soon, he realized that he should not misuse his might on feeble little creatures such as human beings. Life for them was not a sport as it was for him. For them, life meant industry and continued physical labour. He pitied them and hurried towards the west. People sighed in relief as there was no need for them to go in search of a shady place. Shade itself came in search of them. Children broke loose from the clasps of their mothers and ran out of their houses to frolic on the streets.

With utmost patience, Yashodhara watched the eternal passage of time that skilfully moved forward as usual on that day too. She was too drowsy to watch, but she had to watch. The moon would appear only when dusk disappeared. But, when it was time to see him, Yashodhara doubted her purpose for going to the temple. What would she do there except interrupt his meditation? If he were sensible enough, he should take the initiative to start a conversation with her.

Wouldn't it be appropriate for her to wait till he himself made the next move? Such doubts troubled Yashodhara's mind as she had been patiently waiting to meet Siddhartha since she had met him the previous evening. Tears welled up in her eyes. But soon, she realized that it was unnecessary for her to be so anxious since it only gave her pain and not peace. At last, she decided to set out to the temple in search of peace and friendship.

As it was her habit, she was about to venture into the flower garden to the left of the temple, but something stopped her. Siddhartha was waiting at the temple, as if he knew for certain that she would come there. As he looked at her, a gentle smile dawned on his lips, adding splendour to his serene countenance. Yashodhara's courage, which had made her introduce herself to him the previous day, now failed her. She felt shy to look at him and stood there, her head bent down. Siddhartha walked up to her. He stood silently, looking at her for a few minutes.

'Yashodhara,' he said at last with much compassion. 'You wanted to know my name yesterday. You also wanted to know about my parents and my dynasty. Don't you want to know about me? Well, I have come here today to tell you all about myself.'

Yashodhara lifted up her eyes and looked at him. Her looks seemed to ask him what his nature was like.

'Sit there, on that stone slab. I shall stand here and talk to you,' he said.

'Oh, no! How can I? When you stand!' Her voice faltered.

'It's all right. Please be comfortable,' he said.

Yashodhara walked slowly to the stone slab and sat on it. From inside the garden sweet scents, borne aloft by the gentle breeze, rushed to greet them.

'Though I am born in a Kshatriya family, I do not like wars and tests of might. My only desire is to understand deeply the world around me. Except that, no other desire really bothers me. I keep myself away from all worldly affairs in order to understand the world and the pain in it. I am also averse to the religious sacrifices made by the Brahmins. Ordinary people consider me slightly peculiar.'

He stopped and looked at her for a while and then continued.

'I know nothing about you, your hopes and your ambitions. I do not know why you sought me out that day. If you should get disappointed when you perceive my true nature, it's better to get disappointed now, itself.'

Yashodhara looked at him steadily for some time. By then, she was able to overcome her shyness and modesty.

'I have never received the respect you have given me, and I am certain I will never get it from anyone else. I don't wish to lose it. Let me try to understand you. Then, I will be able to understand your exploration of the world. I am sure, I shall never be disappointed with you. I didn't get the opportunity to think so differently about the world as you have. In spite of that, I hate the yagnas and the yagas, and the animal sacrifices. I don't like at all the Vedic precepts. It doesn't mean that I wish to make a philosophical enquiry of the world. I only wish to live peacefully, cherish my self-respect, and never to be insulted for being born a woman. I am sure, I will be able to realize my dreams if I share my life with you.'

Siddhartha was greatly surprised by the clarity, sublimity and prudence with which she spoke. He had never been so close to any other woman except his mother. He had several misconceptions regarding women, and they were all the result of his association with the Sramanas. He heard the Sramanas remark, very often, that women suffer from horrible secret desires. That they ensnare men and make them fall into the pit of family life, out of which it is impossible to escape. That they are selfish and quarrelsome by nature, and it would be better to keep away from them. Siddhartha never tried seriously to verify the veracity of the statements made against women. Now, when he listened to what Yashodhara said, he knew for certain the Sramanas were wrong. He was able to understand that Yashodhara was as unique a person as he himself was.

He went and sat beside her on the stone slab. Their proximity to each other made them feel happy and comfortable. Without the need for words, their hearts, brimming with love, engaged themselves in communion. Slowly the curtain of darkness started descending upon the earth.

Yashodhara was the first to come out of her trance.

'Oh!' she said. 'I haven't collected the flowers yet. I am getting late.'

As she stood up and walked into the garden, Siddhartha followed her. He too chose some flowers and put them in her flower basket. They looked at each other and smiled. They could understand the beautiful secret that when work was done together, it would result in greater happiness than when it was done alone. Though she did not like it, Yashodhara had to bid him farewell and turn homewards. Siddhartha remained there all alone, thinking about his experience with her. By the time his thoughts came to an end, it was time for dinner.

Gotami knew that Siddhartha would be late for dinner. She was not worried about it, in fact, she was much pleased. When Siddhartha looked at his mother, he could understand what she felt about his late-coming.

Suddhodana was in great haste. It looked as if he wanted to free himself from the heavy load of an important task. He had high expectations regarding Siddhartha's marriage, but he was frightened by Siddhartha's disposition and temperament. His experiences with his son, from the beginning, were dualistic in nature. When he was engaged in grand celebrations at the birth of his son, he had to face the tragic reality of the death of his wife. Seven days after the birth of Siddhartha, Mahamaya passed away as if she had come down to the earth only to give him a son. He tried to overcome his grief by showering his love and affection on his son, and truly he was able to overcome it. In order to foster the child, he married Gotami, the sister of Mahamaya Devi. From the day Gotami took the child into her lap, she became not his stepmother but his natural mother. When he looked at the two, mother and child tied up together by the bond of love and affection, he lost his anxiety and became cheerful again.

But what the astrologers said disheartened him again. He now wondered why he had sent for them at all! They predicted that Siddhartha would become either an emperor or a saint. He might give himself over to a life of pleasure and luxury, or he might give up all pleasures and involve himself in work for the well-being of humankind. From that day, he watched his son with utmost attention. As years passed by, he lost the hope that Siddhartha would become a king. At no stage in Siddhartha's growth could he find in him the pride and arrogance associated with the Kshatriya caste. His eyes reflected feelings such as love, kindness, pity and peace. He was well versed in all arts, including the art of fighting, and always excelled in competitions. Yet he learnt them for the sake of learning, and he never had even the slightest inclination to exhibit his expertise.

Suddhodana noticed that Siddhartha liked agricultural work more than any other work. He took Siddhartha to the agricultural fields. But, even there, Siddhartha would get absorbed by the beauty of the fields and the liveliness of the people working there. As he grew older, his engagement with the Sramanas increased, which in turn increased Suddhodana's anxiety. Siddhartha's aversion to feuds and combats with surrounding villages over the distribution of the river water made Suddhodana lose heart. Gotami tried her best to console him, saying that their son was not so stone-hearted as to cause distress to his parents, and that he would surly look after them in their old age. Neither of the two dared to mention the topic of his marriage in his presence. They knew for certain that, if Siddhartha once refused their proposal, they could never hope to convince him again. It made them suppress their agitation and remain silent.

Now Siddhartha himself was thinking about a girl and talked about her with his mother. Suddhodana knew that it was not something to be dismissed, but a matter of utmost importance and urgency. And so he acted in full haste. He made preparations to go to Koliya and visit Bimbanana. He sent a messenger to convey the news of his arrival to Bimbanana, and he sent word to his near and dear ones to accompany him on his errand. The visiting party was much pleased by the warm reception extended by Bimbanana at his residence. But, Bimbanana's silence over the proposal of Siddhartha's marriage with Yashodhara irritated them. After a prolonged, thoughtful silence, Bimbanana revealed to them what was on his mind.

'I have often heard that Siddhartha Gautama doesn't take pride in performing the duties of a Kshatriya. A Kshatriya should defend the members of his family, the people of his village and his followers even at the cost of his life; and for doing it, he should be skilled in sword fighting.'

Suddhodana sighed in relief as his anxiety disappeared at what Bimbanana said. 'My son,' he said with a smile of pride on his lips, 'is well-trained in all kinds of fighting. It is not just learning each of them; he is adept in every one of them.'

Bimbanana was not convinced. 'Every father feels proud of his son's gallantry,' he said, with a sneer on his face. 'My daughter has learnt archery. It doesn't mean she can defend her people.'

'I don't wish to boast about my son. If you are not prepared to believe us, and if you want your eyes be your witness, my son will stand any test to prove his valour,' Suddhodana said, trying to defend his sense of honour. He was not prepared to let go of Yashodhara at any cost.

'Now you have spoken like a Kshatriya,' said Bimbanana. 'I shall make the necessary arrangements for a contest to be held at the outskirts of our villages. When I extend my invitation, you can come with your son and your people. If he wins, Yashodhara, my daughter, will be sent as your daughter-in-law. Otherwise—'

'Stop!' shouted Suddhodana in haste. 'You will not get the chance to complete your sentence.' He stood up and took leave of Bimbanana.

Siddhartha was not pleased by the idea that he should win Yashodhara in a sword-fighting competition. It appealed neither to his ears nor to his heart. Siddhartha listened silently to what his father said and went away without letting his parents know what was on his mind. As Suddhodana and Gotami could read into Siddhartha's silence, they were taken aback. If Siddhartha refused to participate in the competition, Suddhodana would be humiliated for having challenged Bimbanana. More important was that they would have to give up their hopes of getting a daughter-in-law.

Suddhodana felt sorry for upsetting the feelings of his son. Gotami could understand his anguish. 'Siddhartha, no doubt, is very sensitive,' she said, trying to comfort him. 'His mind is like an unfathomable abyss, and we can never see what is in it. His tender heart should get hardened a little. He will not remain forever, I am sure, the child who was moved to tears by a wounded swan. Your attempts to make him a lover of pleasures, without the knowledge of suffering, are in vain. One must undergo suffering. He must learn to face love and hatred, pleasure and pain, joy and sorrow with equanimity. Let him think, let him struggle and let him suffer. Only then the best in him will emerge.'

Gotami made it one of her responsibilities, whenever it was necessary, to make Suddhodana come out of depression with her words of encouragement. By taking up that responsibility, she was able to widen her thought and deepen her wisdom. Women become wiser by taking up the responsibility of their men and guiding them aright, but their wisdom doesn't get exposed to the world. It is confined only to the family. As most men do not like to be guided by the wisdom of their women, some women misuse their intelligence and make their lives miserable. Suddhodana's deep love for his son became his main weakness, and it made Gotami intellectually superior to him. But, compared with that of Siddhartha, her intellect was insignificant. Her knowledge was worldly. Siddhartha was in search of truth. From worldly knowledge, he had just started journeying towards truth. He observed carefully how worldly knowledge, which indeed was necessary for the welfare of the society, would become harmful when it was misused by people who were only worldly-minded. He also observed, on the other hand, the different paths taken by people in the quest for the ultimate truth.

For that reason, it was not as easy for Gotami to convince Siddhartha about something as it was to convince Suddhodana. So, very often, she would withdraw herself from any discussion with Siddhartha. She would listen to him silently and try to understand his thoughts, but it was beyond her imagination to grasp the purity of knowledge he always aspired to gain; and how it would help overcome the pain and sufferings of the worldy life. Yet her faith in him was immense and steadfast.

Even now, Gotami and Suddhodana failed to understand Siddhartha. They knew he was adept at sword fighting, but why he disliked to use it for his personal benefit was beyond their comprehension. Suddhodana's love for Siddhartha made him anxious over his silence, but Gotami's faith in him made her reassure herself that Siddhartha would always do the right thing. The heat of the day made Suddhodana more uncomfortable, while Gotami relaxed with the services of her maidservants.

———

In the garden, some buds were slowly opening up their petals and getting ready to flower, while some were slowly folding up their petals getting ready to wither. Yashodhara's face reflected both their shades and moods. On one hand, she was filled with joy to be in the presence of Siddhartha, and on the other, she was worried by the thought of whether he would be able to win the competition or not.

'It doesn't appeal to my mind at all, Yashodhara,' said Siddhartha placidly, 'that I should compete with all those who wish to marry you and win you. Our living together in wedlock is something to be decided by ourselves.'

Yashodhara was in complete agreement with what Siddhartha said. But he did not stop there. He continued his argument, trying to make his thoughts clearer to her.

'Your father expects me to protect you; to protect the members of my family and also the people of my village. He believes that only someone adept at sword fighting will be able to do it. But, I don't agree with him. What does the word "protect" mean? From whom should I protect? From enemies! Who are those enemies? Why should there be enmity at all? Why should human beings have anger, hatred and enmity for other human beings?'

The depth and intensity of his thoughts made him speechless for a while.

Yashodhara tried hard to understand what he was trying to say, but failed. The idea of protecting someone from animosity was something beyond her grasp. She knew that one should protect oneself or a strong person should protect a weak person from someone filled with animosity. She never thought beyond that, and she did not know if it was possible to think otherwise. That thought was new even to Siddhartha. Until those words had emerged from his mouth, he had not thought deeply over the idea of protection. He wanted to investigate and find out whether it was true and practicable. As Yashodhara was the cause for his new thought, his heart was filled with love for her. He looked at her, and the next moment his love for her was replaced by pity as he found an expression of helplessness on her face. He decided to help her overcome her helplessness, and that decision gave him great strength.

'I know, Yashodhara,' he said regretfully. 'My words must have perplexed and frightened you. I, myself, need to understand them better. But, I am sure, this thought has come into my mind only because of you. Hence, I shall happily take up the responsibility and tell you what I mean. Don't look so desperate.'

Yashodhara's face brightened.

'That means you wish to protect me from my helplessness,' she said with a gentle smile on her face. 'Wasn't that what my father wanted of you? When the members of your family or the people of your village are helpless, you have to take up their responsibility and protect them.'

Gautama laughed heartily. Such laughter was very rare. Like the moonlight of the rising moon on a full-moon night, it captured Yashodhara's heart. She was enraptured by it. Siddhartha was enchanted by her ecstasy, and he helplessly stood staring at her.

Their problem persisted, unresolved. Should they confront Bimbanana and ask him to change his mind? How could it be done? Yashodhara wanted to know the answers. Siddhartha strongly desired to have Yashodhara as his companion, but he was not willing to compete with other suitors and win her. Competitions were not new to him. There were no competitions which he had contested and not won. They were all like child's play for him. Now he was facing the most important event in his life. Marriage for him was not a trifling matter. It was the desire of two mature minds to get united to live together for the rest of their lives. Yashodhara was not a kingdom, not a piece of land, not river water or any other thing or territory to be won in a competition. One should enter into matrimony through love, not through competition.

Siddhartha tried to convince Yashodhara of his point of view in different ways. Such thoughts were new to her, but she grasped their meaning easily. They sparked in her a new awareness. She felt as if her inner spirit, hidden deep in her subconscious mind, had been awakened. Like a flickering flame, it dawned upon her that women had been getting their recognition as human beings because they were able to breathe, because they had bodies, and because they could work. In all other respects, they were treated as things, as valuable property to be possessed by men. She glanced at that flickering light and wished to reach it. But it was too small and too distant. To undertake a journey to reach it would not be easy. The problem concerning her marriage with Siddhartha would have to be solved first. Then she would be able to make that journey not alone, but along with Siddhartha.

Siddhartha too felt that his way of understanding the world around him was undergoing a deep change, and it was all because of Yashodhara. The question, whether women were human beings or things, had never entered his mind till then. Whenever he thought of all human beings as a collective unit, there appeared in his mind only the images of men. He was quite sure that death and disease were common to all people irrespective of their sex, age or creed. But, when he thought of the suffering humanity, there would come into his mind only the images of men. Now, when he was to win Yashodhara in a sword-fighting competition, the question of the identity of women arose. It was a meaningful question. But, who should solve it? Wasn't it Yashodhara's responsibility?

'Can't you tell your father, Yashodhara, that the idea of winning you in a competition doesn't appeal to me?' he said glumly.

Yashodhara looked helpless again, and it made him realize that she was not used to arguing with her father over any issue. 'When there is need for argument, one must argue,' he said again. 'If you feel that the need has arisen now, you should not hesitate to argue. If I can be of any help to you, please let me know.'

Yashodhara could not decide what she should do. She had grown up acknowledging and accepting her father's stubborn attitude. It was his habit to get things done through commands, never through gentle persuasion. Many times, when he ordered her or her mother or the maidservants, she disapproved of his high-handed attitude, even as she obeyed his commands. Her mother had tried, in different ways, to get out of his control. On some occasions, she would shout at him, on some other occasions, she would cry loudly and on special occasions, she would throw and smash all things within her reach. In spite of such manifestations of her resentment, Bimbanana's attitude wouldn't change. It was only very rarely, over matters of no importance, that he listened to her advice. All of this irritated Yashodhara, but she couldn't help it. She knew it was the way of the world. Would it be possible for her, now, to stand before her father with her head held high, look straight into his eyes and argue with him? Could she dare to do it? The very thought of it filled her eyes with tears.

Siddhartha was moved.

'Yashodhara!' he said hastily and remorsefully. 'Don't bother about arguing with your father. Forgive me for trying to overburden you with such a heavy responsibility. I am also responsible for what has happened. I shall talk with your father and make him withdraw his condition.'

Yashodhara wiped her tears and laughed. For a while she got engrossed in deep thought, talking to herself.

'Siddhartha!' she said at last. 'Honestly, the responsibility lies on me. I myself have to prove to him that I am not a trophy or territory that can be won at the end of a competition. If you do that on my behalf, I shall remain to be a thing, not a human being. So don't involve yourself in this. We shall meet again only when the person who has imposed the condition withdraws it.'

Siddhartha could feel and grasp the pride and dignity with which she spoke those words.

He had no personal opinions regarding the self-esteem of women and its need for them. But now, Yashodhara had given him a new eye and also the thought that it was important to look at the world with it. He felt confident that his association with her would help him understand the mysteries of the world better. He felt relaxed. A feeling of equanimity pervaded him like the cool shade of thick foliage.

Both of them were moving about in their own worlds of thought. In spite of their physical proximity, they were far away from each other and were experiencing the loneliness in togetherness. After a long time, Yashodhara stood up to go home. Siddhartha did not want to get separated from her, but at the same time, he felt happy when he noticed that her absence caused him pain.

After she had gone, he stayed there for some more time lost in thought. It pleased him much to think that they would overcome all hurdles and get united. He wanted to find out, when they met again, if she too had that feeling.

Gotami did not get worried at all when she learnt that Siddhartha returned home much after dinner time and went straight to his bedroom. She sent him a few fruits and a glass of milk, and slept peacefully.

Yashodhara decided to talk to her father and oppose his idea of suitors competing for her hand. It was Bimbanana's habit to have his supper within an hour's time after sunset, chit-chat with his neighbours for a while, discuss with his brothers the work to be done the next day and then go to bed. That day, at the end of his routine, when he was on his way to his bedroom, Yashodhara stopped him.

Bimbanana was surprised. He looked at her questioningly.

'Send them word that you wish to withdraw the condition you have imposed this morning, Father,' she said.

Bimbanana failed to get her point immediately.

'What are you talking about, Yashodhara?' he said affectionately.

'I do not wish to become a thing to be won by a brave warrior in a contest. I am prepared to give my wholehearted consent to marry Siddhartha.'

She spoke slowly and firmly, making her father understand that she was quite decisive about what she was saying.

Eventually, Bimbanana was able to see her point. Her attitude not only surprised him but hurt his pride, and he was enraged.

'Giving consent should be done by us, the elders. You are not to involve yourself in such matters.'

Bimbanana tried to control his anger, but his voice sounded loud and harsh.

'I want you to give your consent too. You may refuse to give your consent on any other ground, but not on the doubt that he may not win in a sword-fighting contest. If, by chance, an idiot or a maniac wins, let me make it clear to you, Father, I am not prepared to marry him.'

'Testing the valour and skills of a bridegroom is essential. It's a tradition for Kshatriyas.'

'I have no respect for such traditions.'

Bimbanana could not digest the courage and obstinacy of Yashodhara.

'I am surprised to know that a girl who doesn't respect traditions was born and brought up in my house,' he said.

'It's true, Father. I have scant respect for the duties and traditions of the Brahmins and the Kshatriyas.'

'Then who do you respect?'

'Father, I have come here to talk to you and convince you of my own self-respect. Let me tell you, once and for all, that I am not a prize or a trophy to be won in a contest. I am your daughter, a girl who was brought up with much love and affection by you. If you overlook this fact and stick to your Kshatriya traditions, I shall cease to be your daughter.'

Unable to bear the severity with which she spoke those words, she turned back and sped hastily towards her bedroom.

Bimbanana stood stupefied. He failed to understand how his daughter could speak to him in such a senseless way. Suddenly it struck his mind that, perhaps, his daughter had turned mad, affected by the spell of evil spirits. Did she prattle on about such nonsense in front of others? Wouldn't it be impossible for him to get her married if it was publicly known that she was insane? He was scared by the thought that his daughter would never get married and stay with her parents forever. What a disgrace it would be for him!

It made him tremble, fret and sweat profusely. As he began to think how he would be able to overcome his problem, suddenly a thought flashed across his mind. It brought him hope and courage.

Bimbanana decided to send word to Suddhodana the next morning. He wanted to inform Suddhodana that he was prepared to give his daughter in marriage to Siddhartha without imposing any conditions. He was sure that the news of Yashodhara's madness would not spread overnight. The question of deception would not arise as the proposal of marriage had come from the bridegroom's side.

Bimbanana could not sleep well that night. He did not want to inform his wife that Yashodhara was mentally ill. Perhaps she already knew about it. Perhaps she too was getting scared about it. If she were not aware of it, he needn't frighten her by revealing the secret now. A girl brought up so well – how could such evil thoughts enter her mind?

Bimbanana knew very well that Suddhodana was an honest and respectable gentleman. His wife, Mahaprajapati Gotami, was not the natural mother of Siddhartha, but she had brought him up as if he were her natural son. His own daughter, Yashodhara, would surely get a loving treatment from such a noble lady. On one hand, he was worried about the prospect of Yashodhara's marriage with Siddhartha, and on the other, he was sorry for her pitiable plight.

At the break of dawn, he informed his wife to get prepared to go to Kapilavastu. Visista was aware of the discussions between her husband and Suddhodana about Yashodhara's marriage with Siddhartha. She failed to understand how Bimbanana's decision had changed so suddenly overnight. The expression on his face made it clear that she had no chance of discussing the matter with him. She called Yashodhara, informed her about their visit to Kapilavastu and gave her charge of the duties to be looked after at home.

Yashodhara felt elated at heart and went to attend to the work entrusted to her.

'When fortune favours one, everything will happen to one's surprise and gratification,' thought Suddhodana and Gotami.

The news, that Bimbanana and Visista were arriving to fix Yashodhara's marriage with Siddhartha, made the entire household jump up with joy. Their exuberance crossed all bounds when Bimbanana announced that he was ready to withdraw his condition and celebrate his daughter's marriage with Siddhartha as early as possible. Suddhodana pleased the guests with his courteous reception and sent for his son.

Most of the people on the bride's side had only heard of Siddhartha. Some of them had seen him, but from a distance. Now, when he appeared before them, they were charmed and delighted. His radiant face, his humble and dignified demeanour, his modest and intelligent eyes and his smiling lips, as tender as the petals of a flower, gladdened everyone. A feeling of guilt came over Bimbanana as he remembered his daughter who had turned into a heretic. For a moment, he felt that he was doing gross injustice to the innocent youth before him.

Siddhartha made a low, reverential bow to all and humbly declared that he had no objection to the decision taken by the elders of his family.

Bimbanana compared Siddhartha's respect for the elders with Yashodhara's revolt against him and felt dejected once again.

Gotami and Visista talked dearly about the grand wedding that would soon take place between their children. Gotami explained how sensitive and tender-hearted Siddhartha was, while Visista extolled Yashodhara's capabilities in managing household affairs. When Gotami said that she was eager to see her daughter-in-law, everyone asked her to accompany them on their return journey. She assured them that she would make it convenient to visit Koliya in as short a time as possible.

All those who were close to Siddhartha were greatly surprised by his decision to get married. They wondered how Siddhartha, who was interested in nothing else except meditation, wandering and conversation with the

Sramanas, should accept to get bound by the bond of marriage.

Devadatta and some other youths attacked him with their sharp, arrow-like questions. 'How can you justify what you have done today?'

'What about your quest for knowledge? Will you give it up?'

'Will your love for meditation allow you to love your wife?'

'Will you put an end to your friendship with the Sramanas?'

'Will you ever be able to become a just husband?'

The attitude of the elderly people, however, was different. They congratulated him and remarked that he was, after all, doing something good.

The criticism he received from his friends made Siddhartha dwell upon his decision. He went to Kalamuni's ashram, where he often discussed with Kalamuni questions on epistemology. Kalamuni had recently returned to his ashram after a short tour. He too was anxiously waiting to see Siddhartha again. When he looked at the glum face of the young man, he could at once understand that Siddhartha was in deep trouble. Even after they were seated at their rightful places, Siddhartha remained silent.

'If you share your problem with me, Siddhartha, I shall try my best to help you,' Kalamuni said dearly.

Siddhartha explained to him how his marriage came to be fixed with Yashodhara.

'It's good that you wish to become a householder. What's there to be worried about it? Everything has happened just as you wished it to happen. It should please you,' Kalamuni said gently.

'I know I wish to become a householder. But my inquisitiveness to understand the truth about the creation of the universe, my eagerness to end human sorrow, remain the same even now. I still believe that my life's ambition is to investigate and find the ultimate truth about them. To achieve that goal, I may, perhaps, have to cease to be a householder.'

'What's there to be worried so seriously about it? When time demands it, you can cease to be a householder.'

'It's true, sir. But the thought that I will not be able to answer her tormented heart haunts me.'

'Where is the need to answer? Every man has the right and freedom to cease to be a householder in order to lead the life of an ascetic. It all depends on your will. One may persuade you not to give up family life, but none has the right to prevent you from entering the life of an ascetic. Your decision is important. All shastras proclaim this, and all dharmas accept it. Every man is entitled to achieve the four noble objects of human life. You need not hesitate to sacrifice the duties of a husband in order to achieve the highest end of human life.'

'If I accept to act in accordance with the shastras and dharmas, where is the need, sir, for my investigation? There is a dharma which is superior to all other dharmas, and it says I must be led by the dictates of my conscience. Whether it is about marriage or about renunciation – my decision should be guided by my conscience.'

Kalamuni looked at Siddhartha who remained silent once again. He knew very well that when a man wishes to renounce his family life, he might not always get the permission from his parents. However, their permission is not at all necessary. But why should a man think of taking the permission of his wife? Women entice men and tie them to family life. They would never allow their men to free themselves from the relationship. How foolish it would be to think of taking their consent! They are deficit in matters of spiritual knowledge. They are not eligible for moksha, the liberation of the human soul. They are idiotic and quarrelsome. Frailty is their nature. They know nothing except how to covet and how to seduce men. When men wish to gratify their sexual needs, they get married, and when they wish to gratify their spiritual needs, they give up the relationship. The question of seeking the wife's permission doesn't arise at all even after begetting children.

'You know very well, sir, that I don't accept the superiority of the Brahmins and the Kshatriyas. They have been trying to maintain their superiority by creating the shastras in their favour. People are imprisoned within those dharmas and traditions. It seems to me that every group tries to establish its superiority over some other weaker group hindering the equality of humankind.'

Kalamuni couldn't help but frown deeply.

'Knowledge is pure and abstract. You shouldn't restrict it to the human world and apply it to human beings alone. Unless you liberate yourself from such prejudice, you can't become a seeker of true knowledge.'

'I am a human being. Knowledge, extraneous to the human world, doesn't seem useful to me.'

'Utility is not the purpose of knowledge.'

'Then why should we crave for knowledge which is not useful to us and undergo severe penance for it?

'Knowledge has its own value independent of human interests and utility.'

'I am not convinced by such beliefs.'

'Then, go to those people who promise to lead you to heaven through the shorter routes of performing holy yagnas and yagas. Take to the Vedic ways. They are all centred on human utility and welfare.'

'No, sir. They are all centred on safeguarding the interests of those groups that profess them. If at all there is God, will he allow such selfish people to be his mediators?'

It was usual for them to end their discussion and retire when further conciliatory progress looked impossible.

Kalamuni, too, had no faith in Vedic rituals and in those who mediate between God and human beings. He believed that there was some superior truth and was trying to investigate it. He was patiently waiting to receive the ultimate knowledge about the supreme being. He was involving himself in severe penance and undergoing self-mortification.

Siddhartha took leave of Kalamuni, and on his way home pondered over the question of women. The bitter comments made by Kalamuni against women deeply pained him. He examined himself and wondered if he had ever thought of women collectively as a group, as part of humanity. The revelation, that mankind had so far meant only men for him, surprised and upset him greatly. In the past, he had sometimes given serious thought to the division of people into groups based on caste and its resultant evil. His view, till he had met Yashodhara and faced the problem of winning her in a sword-fighting contest, was that whatever was good or bad for a man was sure to be good or bad for a woman too. But now, he slowly began to realize that what would be good or bad for women was being dictated by men. He wanted to think more seriously and more vividly about women and their individual liberty. He needed more time and much more effort to do so.

However, the immediate problem was different. To solve it, he needed to discuss with Yashodhara. When she learnt about it, she might wisely change her decision. That decision might result in excruciating misery, but in the long run it would turn out to be good for both. They must be truthful to each other. That was very important if they wanted to enter into this new relationship.

That evening, at supper time, Gotami was surprised to find that Siddhartha's mood had changed from what it had been in the morning. That morning his face was bright like the rising sun, but now it looked dull, like the waning moon a couple of days before the moonless night. She felt that he was giving serious thought to something grave. He would tell her if she asked him, but she decided not to ask. She wanted him to churn his mind, to undergo his own mental afflictions and derive an appropriate solution to his problem. After supper, Siddhartha immediately retired to his chamber. Gotami could not bear to see him in such distress. She wiped her moist eyes.

Siddhartha took a decision but, if he disclosed it to Yashodhara, it would deeply agonize her, and that was the real cause for his distress. It was not in his nature to hurt the feelings of anyone, consciously or unconsciously. But now, his conscience told him he had no other option than to hurt her feelings. Truth would always cause pain, but it would only be temporary. If he concealed the truth, he would be considered a cheat and it would become a wound that would hurt her forever. No, he should never hurt her. Hurting anyone for any reason would be cruelty. He should keep her awake and make her aware of the truth. That conviction made him regain his peace of mind.

As Yashodhara did not find Siddhartha in the garden, she went into the temple and saw him sitting at his usual place, immersed in deep meditation. She went and sat in front of him, taking care not to make any noise. His face was radiant, filled with ethereal happiness resulting from deep self-absorption. It was so bright and beautiful that she could not take her eyes off him. As she sat staring at him, she forgot all about herself and her surroundings. She breathed as if she were under some unknown pressure. She did not know when her breath became normal again and when her eyelids slowly drooped shut. But, when she opened her eyes again, she found Siddhartha watching her curiously. Smiling at him, she went and sat by his side.

'When did you come here?' he said, looking at her with affection.

'I don't know. Perhaps I had been here for a long time. Looking at you, I too got transformed like you,' she said.

'In future, Yashodhara, I may get transformed in such a way that it will be impossible for you to follow me,' he said thoughtfully.

Yashodhara was a little perturbed by the tone of his voice. 'What do you mean! How will you change? Why will it not be possible for me to follow you?' she asked innocently.

'I have already told you, Yashodhara, that I am involved in spiritual exploration. Earlier, when I had said I wish to explore the secrets of the universe, you said you wished to explore me. It's fine. But before you get that chance to explore me, let me tell you something explicitly about myself and my inner desires.' He waited for a while to watch her reaction. Yashodhara looked at him, suggesting that he should continue.

'You are well aware, Yashodhara, that I disapprove of the society in which we live, and I think differently from the ways of the world. You said you too were on the same path. Well, to be honest, I don't wish to satisfy myself by just being different and end my exploration there. I want to observe and examine very deeply the society and the well-being of the people in it.'

'Along with it, I want to examine myself and cleanse myself. I wish to reach the extremest ends of human experience, both physical and intellectual. Perhaps my desire to get married and become a householder is a part of it. Yes, it's true. But, if you desire to be my lifelong companion, you may get disappointed. In my quest for knowledge and truth, if I renounce my family, then you will perhaps get submerged in despair. It may be very difficult to bear the pain resulting from the separation. Regarding my parents, I am helpless. That bond comes naturally by birth. When I break it, it is bound to result in sorrow. But we are thinking of forging a new relationship. If we withdraw now, the question of separation and sorrow will not arise. Isn't it my responsibility to make you aware of it? Now, at this moment I consider our relationship to be very dear to me. But, in future it may change.'

Yashodhara, who was listening to him attentively, gave a start and looked worried. 'Our relationship, our love, how can they get altered?'

'Change is inevitable. Every moment is different from its previous moment. Don't you find any change from the day we met for the first time to the present? Please think about it.'

'Yes, there is change. But it resulted in joy.'

'This joy will not remain forever with the same intensity. If my exploration makes me happy, it may cause you pain.'

'What you say grieves me. But somehow I desire to have more of it.'

'If you share your life with me, your grief may grow to be unbearable.'

'Let it grow. I too shall test myself. I too am critical of the society around us, and I too disapprove of its values. I want to find out where your critical outlook will lead you to, and where it will take me. I too am aware of the word truth. I understand its outward meaning only. I am sure, the truth you are in search of is a very different one. I want to share it with you.'

'But, in the process of getting to it, I may not be by your side. Perhaps I will not be.'

Yashodhara sighed deeply. 'Well, let us see how our life unravels. I am introduced to something new because of you. Wherever it may lead me to, I am ready to undertake this journey. Today, you honestly revealed a truth about yourself. I doubt whether such a thing has happened to anyone in the world before. I am inclined to believe that it has never happened. I wish to undergo such experiences though they last only for a few moments. When you are involved in examining the society, I shall engage myself in examining our relationship. I shall receive the knowledge befitting my taste.'

As had happened before, Yashodhara's words introduced to Siddhartha an unknown and unexplored field. They made him understand there was much to think about it.

'I have spoken thus, Yashodhara, not to absolve myself of the guilt I am likely to experience. I felt that it would be better for you to know that we might get separated. Last evening, I heard bitter comments made by Kalamuni against women. I want to know your opinion about them.'

'I don't wish to hear such bitter comments now, at this blissful moment. Our association can wipe off all bitterness from life. I want to enjoy it uninterrupted.'

Siddhartha was moved. He realized all over again that Yashodhara's mind and soul was unique. The life he wished to share with her would be very valuable. He needed her instinct and insight to explore the world. He could feel that she was willing to extend her help to him. His mind was cleared of all its doubts and it was fresh like the clear sky. There, Yashodhara was shining brightly like the queen moon.

As Yashodhara happily narrated her childhood experiences, Siddhartha got submerged in her innocent laughter.

For the first time, he witnessed intellect and innocence living harmoniously in one place.

Was there innocence in him, too? If not, how did his nature take shape so differently from that of others? He walked home, thinking about it.

His mind was ready to take in a new experience of life. His heart was flooded with boundless love for Yashodhara, who had filled his life with thoughts of affection.

A smile of satisfaction appeared on Gotami's face as she discerned the difference that had come over Siddhartha since the previous evening.

She couldn't control her eagerness to go and visit Yashodhara. She got all the necessary arrangements made for her journey to Koliya. The next morning she set out early with valuable gifts to meet her daughter-in-law.

Gotami hugged Yashodhara affectionately. She developed a sense of attachment for Yashodhara, who had miraculously brought about the change they wanted to see in Siddhartha. There was also a feeling of gratitude mixed with it. She gave her daughter-in-law precious ornaments. Looking at them Visista laughed and said, 'When will my Yasho adorn herself with these ornaments? She is not at all interested in such things. Had you given her flowers or birds or sheep, she would have disappeared at once and started playing with them by now.'

Gotami was surprised. She felt it strange that a woman should have no love for ornaments. But at the same time, she also felt that Yashodhara was ideally suited to Siddhartha. What would happen if they were joined in wedlock? She laughed to herself, amused by the thought.

'Our gardens in Kapilavastu can quench your thirst for flowers. And the birds, they will irritate you with their unending twitter. I don't know much about sheep. Your father-in-law will be able to tell you about them,' she said.

Yashodhara smiled at her. She picked up one of the ornaments before her and adorned her neck with it.

'See how she values you and your gifts,' said Visista, staring at her daughter with amusement. 'Had I given it, she would have hidden it at once.'

'These trinkets are no aid to your beauty, Yashodhara. Be yourself. Siddhartha likes to see you that way,' Gotami said, looking at Yashodhara with admiration.

'Oh! A perfect match!' Visista said, laughing aloud.

Yashodhara asked Gotami to tell her all about Siddhartha's boyhood days.

Gotami happily narrated how compassionate Siddhartha was from his childhood, how different he was from the other boys and how he used to try his best to alleviate the pain and sufferings of all beings.

As Yashodhara listened attentively, her heart, too, overflowed with genuine feeling of compassion for all suffering beings. She felt like taking them all into her arms with warmth and affection. Somewhere in the depths of her heart she experienced a strange feeling. She felt that there was nothing else in the world except love and joy, and that there should be nothing else in it.

That wonderful thought brought a new glow to her face. When Gotami noticed it, she experienced, for a moment, an uncanny sensation – a sensation almost like fear. Though it was a fleeting sensation, she was confused by it. She doubted a little whether Yashodhara would be able to mould Siddhartha into the man she wanted him to be.

But Yashodhara, who was more pleasing to her eyes than moonlight, wiped off all her doubts and won her heart.

The way Yashodhara served food made Gotami realize that she would be the most suitable substitute for her. But at the same time she felt sad to face the fact that she would not be able to feed her son for long with her own hands.

'You make me feel that I am going to lose my chance of feeding my son with my own hands,' she said helplessly.

'In that case, you may feed me with your hands,' Yashodhara retorted.

Gotami failed to assess whether Yashodhara was innocent or intelligent. 'I haven't the strength to look after the two of you,' she said.

'Then I shall look after your son and you can look after me. I shall only help you, not burden you.'

Gotami was much pleased by the way Yashodhara beautifully suggested that Siddhartha was going to be her own darling.

'Oh, yes, I would love to. My wish for a son has been satisfied. But for a daughter, it remains. From today, I shall not be bothered by it any more,' she said, taking Yashodhara into her arms.

For the next few moments, Yashodhara rested peacefully in those arms which had affectionately tended Siddhartha since his childhood.

Looking at the two, Visista's eyes filled with tears. Her daughter, embracing someone else as she would embrace her own mother, pleased and displeased her at the same time. She left the place as if she had some important work to attend to.

Gotami had learnt from Siddhartha everything in detail about his first and second meetings with Yashodhara. Now she felt like asking her to tell her all about their other meetings. But she held back, thinking that it was neither the proper place nor time. She knew that Yashodhara would reveal it when she came to Kapilavastu as Siddhartha's wife. The purpose for which she had come to Koliya was fulfilled. Now it would be proper for her to leave. In her heart, she longed to be with Yashodhara for some more time. It made her realize how difficult it would be for Siddhartha to stay away from her. She advised Visista to decide on the auspicious date for their wedding as soon as possible.

Visista expressed her helplessness in that matter. She said that it all depended on her husband's decision. Yashodhara, however, was not pleased and convinced with her mother's opinion.

'Don't say that, Mother,' she intervened. 'In the past you used to say that the ultimate authority when it would come to my marriage would always be my father. But now you have seen for yourself how I was able to win over his authority. We, too, have power over men. We, too, can exercise our authority. What we need is to understand that we have power. It's just that.'

She turned to Gotami and said, 'Don't get worried. Our wedding will take place very soon.'

Once again Gotami was thrown into a state of confusion. She felt that Yashodhara was not so innocent as she appeared outwardly. She had depth of character. Dignity, innocence and peacefulness were only her external characteristics. What her real nature was would only be known with the passage of time. She felt for certain that Yashodhara was fit to be the companion of Siddhartha. She would not be disturbed by his whims and fancies. On the contrary, she would give him the strength of mind to make right choices.

'Yashodhara's union with Siddhartha is most unusual – the rarest of rare events,' she thought.

She knew how happy Suddhodana would feel if she told him all about Yashodhara. Her eagerness to tell him everything that happened in Koliya made it possible for her to bid farewell to Yashodhara and return to Kapilavastu. All along the way, from time to time, she wiped her tears of joy. Till the previous day, Siddhartha's marriage was a dream for his parents. But now it was reality.

The elders of the two families celebrated the marriage as if it were a festival. Suddhodana knew well that Siddhartha was averse to marriage rituals and so he saw to it that there would be as few rituals as possible at his house.

Bimbanana, who had high regard for Vedic rituals, followed all traditional rituals of marriage as upheld by the Brahmin priests. Yashodhara could see that Siddhartha was getting vexed during the rituals. She advised him in whispers not to get bothered but to entertain himself by looking at the priests conducting the foolish and ridiculous acts. She said she was doing the same to ease her mind. It would be very difficult to control one's laughter and she was, throughout the course of rituals, trying her best to overcome that difficulty.

Yashodhara's attitude surprised Siddhartha. As he followed her advice, he was relieved of his vexation and its place was taken up by joy. For some time, he delighted himself secretly observing Yashodhara and her attempts to control her laughter. But his mind was so used to thinking and analysing things that, after a short time, it started searching for the meaning of what she had said. At what stage of intellectual development would it be possible for one to laugh at something that vexes the mind?

Anger and vexation fill the mind with hatred. He knew that he disliked Vedic traditions and the rites and rituals associated with them. He never thought they could be changed in his favour, for his benefit. What did Yashodhara mean when she asked him to laugh at them? When one understood their uselessness, and laughed at them without regard, one would be filled with a sense of amusement in place of hatred. One's heart would be lightened. Laughter would make us reach the next higher step of vexation. Yet, was it really the higher step? If one learnt to laugh at the follies of human beings and bear falsehood, how would it be possible to change them? What exactly was Yashodhara's suggestion? Was she asking him to laugh and bear or was she asking him to laugh and then change? He failed to understand to what intellectual stage she had reached. Was it that of an innocent child or a mature human being?

By the time Siddhartha came out of his thoughts, all the remaining rites of marriage had been finished, and the elders were coming forward to bless them.

That evening Yashodhara bade farewell to the village where she was born and brought up. She said goodbye to her parents, relations and friends. She held Siddhartha's hand and set out to Kapilavastu in search of her future life. She wiped the tears of her parents and comforted their hearts laden with sorrow. She asked in a mild tone of rebuke why they, who had taught her from her childhood that a girl must leave the house into which she was born, were weeping? Her parents were moved by her words and wept more bitterly.

For Siddhartha, the scene was intolerable. He thought about Yashodhara and her parents. She had to move away from her parents because she married him. It made her parents miserable. She didn't look so miserable but she must have felt it in her heart. What did it mean? They celebrated the marriage knowing well that it would cause suffering. If something done willingly resulted in suffering, what would be the degree of pain caused by something done unwillingly?

Suddhodana and Gotami felt it difficult to hurry them and make them get into their vehicles. After getting into their carriage, Siddhartha sat beside Yashodhara, took her hand into his and said, 'Yasho, do you feel sad?'

Yashodhara smiled with tears in her eyes and said, 'I can't say I am not sad, but at the same time I am happy. Perhaps my happiness is greater. No, not perhaps. It is.'

With love and affection, he pressed her hand and put it on his heart. 'Your departure and the ensuing separation pained your parents much,' he said.

'They have dreamt of this day since my birth. They have been eagerly waiting for it. It is all a part of life. By now, my mother would have forgotten her pain. She will be trying to set right all things that must have got jumbled up because of my marriage. My father will be proudly narrating to all those gathered in front of his house how grandly he celebrated his daughter's marriage. Everyone at home will be happily talking about our marriage.'

The way Yashodhara explained the situation made Siddhartha smile satisfactorily. 'It's all right with them. But what about you? How do you feel at heart?'

'As we move away from my village, I feel light at heart. I am about to begin my new life. I am glad that I have found a companion with whom I can share my thoughts without any inhibition. My desire to taste your love is growing stronger.'

As her face became bright with joy, Siddhartha experienced boundless love for her. He was so pleased to be so close to her that he wished to be with her all alone forever. Whenever the carriage jolted a little, they were brought closer and closer.

Gotami told everyone as if she were making an important announcement that the house had become Yashodhara's from the moment she stepped into it. Very old and disabled people who had not been able to attend the marriage were eagerly awaiting her arrival.

Now they went and saw her. They blessed her, gave and received gifts, dined and returned home, much pleased. Yashodhara moved along with Gotami, assisting her in every work. It seemed as if she had been living in that house for many years and was accustomed to all its traditions and routines.

'You are tired, Yashodhara. Now, you must listen to me. Go and rest. Don't let people say that I made you work hard from the first day itself.'

Gotami chided Yashodhara with graceful affection and sent her into Siddhartha's room.

Siddhartha was in a deep sleep as he was too tired to keep himself awake till she came. As she did not like to disturb him, she went and lay by his side and slept peacefully.

Very early the next morning when he awoke, Siddhartha found Yashodhara fast asleep beside him, and he could not take his eyes off her. There was a faint smile on her lips which was as pleasant as the smile of an innocent, newborn child. She had removed all her ornaments. Her long black hair was spread all over her back. The hair was decorated with a thin garland of white flowers. Clad in soft silks, she looked divine. The thought that she was sleeping by his side throughout the night made him experience inexplicable joy. He sat staring at her until daybreak.

When Yashodhara's eyes opened, Siddhartha's face delighted them. She smiled sweetly. She got up from bed, adjusted her clothes, knotted her hair, removed the garland of flowers, put it around Siddhartha's neck and left the room.

Still in trance, Siddhartha's eyes just noticed her actions without any reaction.

Though Yashodhara had gone, the sweet scent of her body still lingered in the air, and it touched him softly, making the day lovelier for him. It took him quite long to come out of his trance, and when he came out of it, he began to think deeply about the emotional state he had reached. He waited for some time, expecting Yashodhara to return, and finally moved out to attend to his household duties.

It was unanimously agreed upon that the house had become more elegant and more graceful with the arrival of Yashodhara.

The way she moved about the house smiling, the way she decorated the house with flowers, and the way she did every work she could get hold of, while concentrating her thoughts on Siddhartha, brought grace to the house.

Anyone who looked at Siddhartha could easily understand that he enjoyed his association with Yashodhara. Though he wanted to spend all his time in her company, he reserved a little for meditation and a little more for discussions with the Sramanas. Soon, his life got so naturally entwined with her life that there was no cause for worry or need for any sort of artificial adjustment. That was how Yashodhara took him into her life and got united with his life. Whether the other people noticed it or not, Gotami and Siddhartha were able to notice it. Gotami felt happy about it and remained silent. But Siddhartha could not.

'Yasho! How did it all happen?' he said, trying to free himself of a hypnotic state.

'Don't you think it's all my doing?' said Yashodhara, feeling a little elated.

'I am trying to know why it all happened this way,' he paused to muse.

'You should not think when it is time for you to sleep. You can think about it tomorrow at your leisure.'

Yashodhara gently closed his eyes with her soft palms.

His eyes were closed but his mind was awake, and it was thinking.

He knew he was happy. He also knew that his happiness wouldn't remain the same forever. Separation and suffering were inevitable. Love, union, disunion and depression are all bonds – human bonds. Entangled with such bonds, human beings fail to free themselves from suffering. What could be the source of such bonds? How to avoid the suffering caused by them? Would it be possible to find a way to end suffering? Siddhartha had seen and met many scholars, ascetics and Sramanas, but none of them seemed to be searching for such a way. Perhaps, they were not in pursuit of answers to such questions. But he, who made the quest for true knowledge the object of his life, was also bound by the bonds of love and affection. Now, at this stage of his life and investigation, Yashodhara might not become a bond and cause him suffering. But sometime in future, it would surely plunge him in pain.

'What are you thinking about? Won't you tell me?' Yashodhara said.

'I am afraid, Yashodhara, your love may become a bond and cause us suffering sometime in future,' he replied.

Yashodhara laughed lightly and said, 'No. That will never happen.'

'But, on that day when my heart orders me to set out on my investigation, how will you react?'

'Till you receive such an order, let the waves of your thought touch my heart. Then I, too, will be able to give you that order.'

Siddhartha was astonished at Yashodhara being so attuned to his feelings.

'Time and again, you have been telling me about the questions that trouble your mind. I too think about them. But you never share with me what you have discussed with the Sramanas and other scholars,' she said, trying to make him feel comfortable.

'I thought you wouldn't understand them,' he said.

'It is your responsibility to teach me. You have been searching for an honest and rational way to rid the world of suffering. When you find it and wish to teach it, isn't it your duty to make ordinary people like me understand it?'

Siddhartha gaped at her for a while.

'I feel that I have not understood you so well as you have understood me,' he said.

'Yes, you are right. It's because I have only you to observe and think about. But you have the whole world before you. In it you see innumerable people leading wretched lives without knowing why their lot has been so unfortunate. That perhaps is why you take more time to understand me,' she said and smiled at him beautifully.

Siddhartha decided, on the spot, that he should make her his companion in his investigation of the eternal truth. From that day, he started spending even the evening time with her.

Gotami and Suddhodana were quite happy to see the steady change in their son. But they were unable to understand the change that was coming over Yashodhara. The brightness and peace in her face, they thought, was the result of her intimacy with Siddhartha. It was true. But they failed to realize that their intimacy had brought change in both, and that change was making their intimacy stronger.

One evening, Siddhartha told Yashodhara Kalamuni's opinions about women.

Yashodhara listened, smiled and remained silent.

'Until recently I did not think of women as a separate group. Isn't it foolish to say that all women are the same, and that they think and act in a similar vein? What stupidity!' he said in disgust.

'Yes, but stupidity will be treated as wisdom when there is no one to explain that it is foolish to hold such opinions.'

'You are right. Many things pass off as valid when there is no contrary opinion. It is also foolish to divide people into groups based on the work they do, and to consider some groups as mean and inferior. Nobody cares when we say it is unjust. They don't wish to look at the truth.'

'Yes, the same can be said about yagnas and yagas.'

'Isn't it funny to say that priests are the mediators between God and human beings? My conscience doesn't accept the idea of God – a god responsible for the creation of all that is animate and inanimate in the universe.'

'Conscience is a poor witness. We need solid proof. Show it,' Yashodhara challenged him.

'What exists can be proved. What doesn't exist can't come forward to claim that it doesn't exist,' he said helplessly.

Yashodhara couldn't help laughing and Siddhartha joined her.

Those who heard them laugh did not know the seriousness of the joke. They smiled at each other mischievously.

'As women are confined to their homes, their intellectual growth gets stunted. If they get a chance to talk to people like you, they will get new ideas and their intellect will blossom. But they never get such opportunities. Some women, however, learn even though they are bound by their homes. See how your mother, Gotami, has brought up a son like you. She has provided an atmosphere which is most suited to your intellectual growth. She didn't consider you to be stubborn or irrational. She thought you were distinct, and she tried to safeguard your distinctions. Imagine how intelligent a woman should be to understand that. There may be many such capable women in the world. But they won't come out and make their capabilities known to all. Perhaps they don't wish to be considered special or exemplary.'

'But you wish to be, don't you? It's enough. It must get started somewhere. Only then the truth about women will get proved.'

'Truth will come to light only though you. You love all creatures in the world and think about them affectionately.'

Siddhartha hesitated for a while to say something and finally came out with it. 'It hurts me to know that you deprive flowers of their life.'

'Really! In that case, you should go into the garden after I finish decorating the house with flowers and see for yourself what you find there,' Yashodhara said expressing affected displeasure at his comment.

'Sure,' he said, 'I will go and see. But won't you tell me first what I shall find there?'

'No. I won't. Some things are meant to be heard and known, others to be seen and known.'

'Is that so? You won't tell me, then. It's all right. But even if you won't tell me and even if I don't go and see, I can understand what it is. Yes, I know the truth.'

A victorious smile appeared on Siddhartha's lips.

'You know the truth! What is it? Tell me, quick.'

'Can't you understand it looking at my face? Do I need to tell you?'

'I can. But I don't have that much patience now. I am too impatient to wait and think. Come on, out with it. What have you understood?'

'The truth is that you don't pluck flowers. You just gather those that have dropped down to the ground. You don't deprive them of their life; you add a new meaning to their lives which, otherwise, get wasted. That is the whole truth, isn't it?'

Yashodhara looked at Siddhartha with her eyes wide open and full of admiration.

In appreciation of her beautiful eyes Siddhartha said, 'But I don't like you to pluck the lotus flowers in the pond, remove their petals and stick them to your eyes.'

Siddhartha made his comment in such a serious mood that it took quite some time for Yashodhara to grasp its meaning, and when she understood what he meant by it, she laughed aloud heartily.

'I am beginning to think that you have a better hold on poetry than on philosophy. Why don't you try your hand at it?' she teased him.

'Poetry and philosophy emerge from the emotional experiences of the heart. Somewhere, they must become one. But sadly, poetry has become a tool to publicize superstitious ideas and sensual pleasures. This too is something to be thought about seriously.'

The way Siddhartha turned a trivial joke into a philosophical discourse surprised Yashodhara.

'There is nothing in this universe which is unfit for your perception. How wide your mind should be to accommodate all things in it,' she said in admiration.

'It may be infinitely wide, but it's of no avail. These days, all things fail to enter it as its whole space is occupied by one person.'

Though he spoke the words in a dull, dismal tone, Yashodhara could catch the jest at once.

'An exaggerated untruth, though sweet and pleasant, doesn't sound splendid when spoken by Siddhartha,' she said pretending to be angry. 'Come, let's go. It is time we did something more useful. Tonight, you must tell me all your thoughts.'

Yashodhara came to know from the maidservants that one of the women in the village had committed suicide by jumping into the river Rohini as she was regularly beaten and abused by her husband. She was deeply moved and agitated. It was not the first time she had heard about wives being ill-treated by their husbands. When she was young, she had seen her mother being beaten by her father twice. Both times she had wept bitterly. Those memories still haunted her imagination. As she grew older, she used to get disheartened whenever her friends or maidservants reported of wife-beating. It was the main cause for her reluctance to get married.

At that time, she had no one with whom she could discuss such matters. Everyone talked as if it were natural. None considered it to be unjust.

Now she had Siddhartha.

What Yashodhara said was not new to him.

There were occasions when some of the elders, teachers and saints, with whom he discussed the matter, had said, 'Women are brutes. They deserve such treatment.'

Whenever he heard such bitter comments, Siddhartha felt much annoyed. He used to oppose those people and go away from them.

When he told her about some of those occasions Yashodhara reacted severely.

'If women are brutes, isn't it necessary to treat them much more kindly?' she said.

Without looking at the logic of her words and without justifying her statement, Siddhartha proceeded to say that one should understand first that women are not brutes.

They talked at length of people who beat cattle, hunt innocent animals and birds, and torture and abuse women.

In the course of their conversation, Siddhartha mentioned that once he saved the life of a wounded swan.

Yashodhara wanted to know about it in detail. For Siddhartha, that day was unforgettable.

He could always recall his feelings of pity and love that were aroused in him by a wounded bird, and the bliss he experienced by nursing it back to life. He narrated the incident so meticulously that Yashodhara felt as if everything was happening before her eyes.

A swan, flying in the sky, fell to the ground when it was hit by an arrow shot by Devadatta, Siddhartha's cousin. The bird, severely wounded and bleeding, was struggling to fly again, but it couldn't. Looking at the wound and the blood, Siddhartha trembled with fear and anxiety. He had never experienced severe physical pain except for that caused by the bruises he received during games. Now, when he looked at the bird wriggling and writhing with pain, he could understand that it was not ordinary pain, but something tied up to its life and its existence.

As the bird looked at him, its eyes filled with fear and agony, his own fear eased, and he began to worry what he should do with it. When the bird screeched, as if it were begging 'Help me, oh! Help me', it suddenly occurred to him what he should do.

He bent down and carefully took the bird into his hands. He could feel its heart beating very rapidly. There was a trickle of blood coming out from the wound. Siddhartha passed his hand over the bird gently, and caressing it he walked up to a nearby pond. His left hand sheltered it while the right hand gently brushed its back.

By the time he reached the pond, the swan's heartbeat seemed to have softened. He could feel that the bird trusted him and took him for a friend, and he felt very happy. 'Is there so much peace and security in the belief others form of us that we are their friends?' he thought.

The swan wriggled with pain in his hands as he washed its wound with the fresh, cool water of the pond. In a short time, blood stopped oozing from the wound and Siddhartha hurried back to his house, where he found a soft cloth to bandage the wound with. He then made the bird lie on a soft mattress.

The swan, which was very weak and tired, closed its eyes and tried to rest as it felt safe. Siddhartha sat by it, stroking its back gently with his palm. He could feel its heart beating slowly but steadily. He felt sure that it would recover in a few hours.

When the bird opened its eyes, Siddhartha placed some food and water before it. The bird was filled with a sense of gratitude. It showed its love and affection by gently rubbing its beak on his palms. Siddhartha's heart was filled with pleasure. He realized that true happiness could be derived only through service rendered to the weak and the needy.

The eyes of the swan became bright and lively when its hunger and thirst were satisfied. 'What a change in a short time of two hours!' thought Siddhartha. He observed how pain and hunger belong to the physical plane while fear and doubt dwell deep in the mind. Now its body and its mind were refreshed. It looked at Siddhartha as if it were trying to say that it could easily bear the pain now.

When Siddhartha removed the bandage and applied some medicine on the wound the bird could bear the pain and cooperate with him.

It dawned upon Siddhartha's mind that it would be easier to bear pain than bear fear and doubt. If the two are removed and love is assured, it would help to heal any wound in a shorter time.

As the treatment continued and as the swan recovered a little each day, Siddhartha could not only observe but also feel the change that was coming over the bird. The sense of belonging with which the bird looked at him and touched him made him extremely happy. Feeding the bird, applying medicine to its wound, watching it regain its strength and walk by itself – when such work gave him so much pleasure he could not understand how others derived pleasure by hurting or killing other beings?

Devadatta and many of his friends hunted small animals like rabbits and also birds. They took into their hands the wounded animals, looked at them with much pride and satisfaction and laughed at them as they wriggled with pain and trembled with fear. Their pleasure, too, was real. No one could deny it. But he too experienced pleasure by protecting the swan from fear and pain. Was there any difference between the two? If there was any, what was the nature of that difference?

Siddhartha could not find an answer and he turned to his mother for help. At first, Gotami was perplexed by his question. She wondered how such a young boy as Siddhartha could think of such grave problems. She herself had no idea of the difference between the two kinds of happiness. But Siddhartha was looking at her, expecting an answer.

'Their happiness is only mischief, my dear,' she said. 'It's not like your happiness.

'Yours is good, not theirs.'

That answer did not satisfy Siddhartha. He knew that she was helpless, and he did not want to trouble her.

'You are right, Mother,' he said. 'I feel better when I offer help.'

Later, he posed the question to his teacher. The teacher was very fond of Siddhartha.

He made him sit on his lap and affectionately stroked his head.

'I can't clarify your doubt, Siddhartha,' he said. 'But I shall express my thoughts about it. Listen to what I say and keep on thinking about it. Perhaps in future you will be able to find an appropriate answer. Then, if I am alive, you must enlighten me with it. You see, we, human beings, are born with different kinds of nature. We develop different kinds of tastes, based on our exposure to things around us. How and why such differences are present, and how they can be removed, I do not know. It is true that there is variety and it is also true that there is both beauty and ugliness in the variety. Most people in the world derive pleasure by causing pain to others. In my life, till now, I have found only you, the other way round. How wonderful the world would be if all people could think and act like you. But it is impossible. I think the human race is getting habituated to deriving pleasure through violence. If the world has more number of people like you who are capable of showing genuine love for the suffering, our lives will become happier and more meaningful.'

Yashodhara, who was completely absorbed in what she was listening to, suddenly gave a start.

'What! Is the world getting habituated to violence?' she asked.

Her lips trembled. Her voice faltered. She moved closer to Siddhartha and reached for his hand. Siddhartha held her hand gently but firmly and tried to pacify her agitated heart with his explanation.

'It seems so, Yasho,' he said quietly, almost as if he were talking to himself.

'In order to put an end to that habit, we have to bring about a great change in human nature. We must be able to prove that the pleasure we get through violence is not really pleasure. It is an illusory pleasure, an erroneous representation of happiness, caused by the fickleness of the mind. Everywhere, I see people getting addicted to violence. The world is increasingly getting filled with such addicts who passively suffer from it and fail to get out of that mire. They must be made to understand how vile and sickening the acts of violence are. They must be made to realize that love and pity for the weak and the suffering are nobler traits. Hunger, pain and misery are ailments which should arouse feelings of pity and sympathy in us. If we do not react to the suffering of others, it only means that there is something wrong with us. Just as we need medical aid to remove physical illness, we also need spiritual thought to remove the illness of the mind. Unfortunately, spiritual thought is misunderstood and mixed up with worshipping God and the achievement of personal deliverance. That concept misleads the world. To me spiritual thinking means to inculcate the qualities of love, kindness and compassion in the hearts of people. Showing tolerance towards others and cooperating with others are real spiritual values. All people have spiritual needs, Yashodhara, but they do not understand them. Before they understand them, they are introduced to meaningless religious practices. They are made to believe that following superstitious customs is a pathway to spirituality. These religious sacrifices and oblations to gods make people insensitive to human suffering. We should introduce love, pity and compassion to such people. We must make them savour the sweetness of these noble qualities. It is a tremendous work that has to be taken up and done simultaneously by many.'

'But how many understand its importance?' Yashodhara felt dispirited.

'We, the two of us. In the past I thought I was alone. But now as I know you are with me, I feel strong and enthusiastic to take up this work.'

The words spoken by Siddhartha, so heartily and so earnestly, made Yashodhara's heart dance like a wave.

They sat there silently for a long time dreaming of a world where nothing else but love and compassion dwelled. They enjoyed the company of each other to the contentment of their hearts.

Gradually, gravity and profundity of thought replaced fun and jest in their conversation. Sometimes Yashodhara would sit with Siddhartha until the last lights of the evening slowly disappeared into the darkness of the night. Even then, when she tended to her household work, she looked as if her mind was elsewhere. The other women of the household kept away from her because of her serious disposition. Gotami observed her carefully. She felt anxious and worried that Siddhartha was perhaps disappointing her with his cold and indifferent demeanour. She had seen how Yashodhara was able to kindle the flame of love in his heart and she firmly believed that their love would bring into the house a new child who would draw Siddhartha's attention much more strongly than Yashodhara could draw. The bond of conjugal love might get weakened with the passage of time, but a father's love for his son would keep on growing, forever fresh, forever new. If Siddhartha tasted that fatherly love, they could all rest in peace. But when would it happen?

Gotami decided to discuss the matter with Yashodhara. 'Poor soul!' she thought to herself. 'She has been bearing a lot of pain all by herself. Her mental pressure must be eased. But will it be possible for Yashodhara to talk about her personal, marital affairs with her mother-in-law? Won't she feel embarrassed? A well-brought-up woman will never wish to make complaints against her husband to his mother. However, a daughter will be able to open her heart and discuss all her troubles with her mother. If Yashodhara tells her mother what exactly is the worry with Siddhartha, she will be able to learn it from her. But Yashodhara has not even talked of visiting her parents since her arrival. It looks as if she has completely forgotten them. In that case, I myself must find an excuse to send her to Koliya.'

Gotami sighed in relief as she had been able to find a suitable solution to her problem.

After the moon had risen in the sky, Yashodhara made arrangements for dinner and waited for Siddhartha.

A maidservant came and told her that Gotami wanted to see her. Yashodhara felt that her mother-in-law had something important to tell her; otherwise she wouldn't send for her at that hour. So she hurried anxiously to see her.

Yashodhara felt greatly relieved when Gotami received her affectionately and made her sit beside her.

Gotami learnt from Siddhartha how one should convey one's ideas directly without beating about the bush.

'Yashodhara!' she said gently. 'You are my daughter. There is no doubt about it. As a mother, I can understand how anxiously another mother will be looking forward to the arrival of her daughter who is away from her. Why don't you go and visit your mother just once?'

Yashodhara was moved. Her face turned pale and tears trickled down her eyes.

Gotami wiped them.

'Why didn't you tell me you did want to see your mother? Why do you suffer in silence? Won't you share your sorrow with your mother? Aren't I your mother?'

Gotami tried to comfort her.

Yashodhara wiped her eyes herself and laughed.

'You are my mother. There is no exaggeration about it. It is exactly for that reason I am not nostalgic about Visista Devi who, according to you, is my natural mother. I don't wish to leave this house and go anywhere. I cast off my modesty to tell you that every moment I live with your son is valuable to me. I need not tell you that he is the noblest of men born into this world. No one, not even you, can understand how rare and extraordinary my association with Siddhartha is. We maintain a regular communion with each other even when we are not together. Here and now, when I am with you, I converse with him. I love to talk to him, look at him and enjoy his presence. But you know it is not always possible. Anyway, I am not going anywhere. Please, don't feel anxious about me.'

Gotami failed to understand what exactly Yashodhara was hinting at. The association she was talking about seemed rare, even extraordinary. It belonged to the spiritual plane, surely not to the physical. Would it mean that there had been no physical union between the two? She could not make out whether Siddhartha was under the influence of Yashodhara or if it was the other way around. Suddenly, she remembered something she wanted to ask her. What she intended to know might not get materialized because she asked about it. It all depended on the will of God. But she must make sure whether Yashodhara had turned her attention towards it or not.

Gotami could not control her curiosity any longer.

'You see, my daughter,' she said softly. 'Seasons have been turning since your marriage with Siddhartha. Your body has been responding well to the periodical changes that occur in nature. I believe it gives a woman so much pleasure when she goes against nature and pauses her menstrual period. I hope you understand what I say.'

Yashodhara laughed. There was shyness mixed with modesty in her laughter.

'It has to take place as naturally as the setting in of seasons. When it has to set in, it will set in. Don't think much about it, Mother,' she said.

'How can I stop thinking about it? Your father-in-law and I have been ardently waiting to see our heir. It is your responsibility to fulfil our dreams. Don't neglect it. Motherhood is a wonderful experience. If you are mentally prepared for it, your body will follow suit. You are wise enough to know your duties well. What more can I tell you?'

Yashodhara sat there for some time, head bent down and lost in thought. Then she stood up and walked slowly out of the room.

Gotami couldn't understand what exactly Yashodhara's response was and her anxiety persisted.

'I have done what all I can do about it. The rest depends on destiny,' she said to herself.

The Koliyas and the Sakyas were getting ready for a battle to settle the issue of sharing the waters of the Rohini. The news roused passions and built tension among the people in all villages along the river. As there was sufficient rainfall for the past two or three years, the problem of sharing river water did not crop up. Every time the rains failed, the issue had to be settled through a battle, on a small or large scale.

During such times Siddhartha used to tell his father and the elders of his village that they should pacify the people through means other than physical confrontation and maintain peace. War could never yield a positive result. But those people, who were incensed by prejudices, would never understand the noble teachings of young Siddhartha.

Some called him innocent. Some others accused him of timidity. But they all joined hands to fight out the issue. Some died in battle while others returned badly wounded or with loss of limbs. They developed a deeper grudge against their opponents responsible for their misfortune. Those who survived with minor injuries talked proudly about their valour, or listened with pride and satisfaction when others eulogized their sacrifices.

Such things always made Siddhartha uneasy and restless.

Now, when he heard the news of the impending danger, he lost his peace of mind. Yashodhara was also deeply agitated. The people on both sides were her kith and kin.

It would not be possible to predict who would die and who would survive. 'Is there no way to prevent this sinister battle?' she thought.

Suddenly she remembered Siddhartha and her face brightened. Siddhartha who always thought about peace and non-violence – wouldn't he be able to prevent that battle? He possessed that potential. If only he tried, he would surely succeed.

In high spirits, she went looking for Siddhartha. She found him lost in thought, uncertain about his course of action. With a pat on his shoulder, she brought him back to the present moment and told him to get ready to prevent the unwanted war.

'It is easy to go and fight a war,' said Siddhartha meekly, the tone of his voice expressing his helplessness. 'To fight a war you just need to go with a weapon into the battlefield. There you fight on one side and win over the other. Preventing a war is different. It is fighting with both sides and winning over both sides. That is very hard. Don't misunderstand me, Yashodhara. I am deeply concerned about it. Time and again, I have apprised the elders in their assembly at length of the devastating and distressing effects of war.

'They call me a timid child. They laugh at me and heckle my words of advice. These people have been so strongly provoked that they have gone mad about war. It is fanaticism at its highest and there seems to be no cure for it. I fear these wars, one day, will lead to the annihilation of humans. We forget we are human beings. We become insensitive to the finer feeling of life. We injure one another; we kill one another; we feel delighted at the sight of blood and laugh wildly at the pain of others. This hysterical madness for bloodshed is the most dangerous of all kinds of insanity. But, at the same time, it is the most attractive of all. I do not understand why human beings discriminate between "us" and "them" and are possessed by bloodlust. We do not know how and when we as a race got contaminated by such sadistic pleasures. Nobody thinks of putting an end to it. The alluring ideas, woven around war, make the human race face the imminent danger of being swept away.'

As Yashodhara listened to him, she turned wild with emotion and spoke to him in a stern, authoritative tone.

'Siddhartha Gautama!' she said looking straight into his eyes. 'You have to stop this war. You, only you, can stop this war. Till now you have been treated as a youngster and paid deaf ear in the assembly of elders. It's true you are young, but your wisdom is mature and ripe. Now, take my word and walk into the battlefield with your weapon of ahimsa. Stand between the two opposing groups. Address them loudly; voice your thoughts on love, pity, compassion and peace. Let your message of peace make them drop down their arms and withdraw from the battlefield. You can do it. Go!'

She spoke with such unswerving faith and confidence in Siddhartha's ability to prevent the war that Siddhartha set out at once, his face aglow with the light emanating from his vehement resolve.

When Gotami heard the news that Siddhartha was going to the battlefield, all alone and unarmed, she ran out to meet him and prevent him from stepping out of the house.

Yashodhara intercepted her. 'Don't think of this as ominous, Mother,' she said. 'Your son is going to stop the war, not to fight it. Believe me, he will return victorious.'

Gotami felt that Yashodhara had gone mad.

'Do you think they will pay heed to the words of a youngster and give up their arms? What do you know about these warmongers? They are like man-eating tigers; they won't leave him.'

'You must really look forward to the day when people will not leave Siddhartha. Give him your blessings, Mother. That day will surely come. This is just the beginning. He will win over the hearts of people on both sides with his noble teachings of peace as his weapons!'

Everything became clear to Gotami now. She realized that Yashodhara had become involved in the philosophical interests of Siddhartha and was encouraging him. She shuddered to think what would happen in the future if it went on. What was this girl going to do? Suddenly she felt very weak. Trembling with fear, she fainted.

With the help of a few maidservants, Yashodhara took Gotami to her bedchamber and made her recline on the bed. After she had regained a little strength, Yashodhara left her to the care of the maids and retired. She went and stood at the main gateway, eagerly waiting for Siddhartha's return.

She was unaware of the passage of time. Morning changed into noon. The sun hesitated to burn brightly on that day. Before the day turned cool, the wind stopped blowing. As it became oppressively sultry, Yashodhara began sweating profusely. It appeared as if she would collapse unless a cool breeze blew over her at once.

Just then the weather began to change. The wind moved gently towards her, carrying with it some pleasant words.

'The battle was not fought. Both sides surrendered to Siddhartha's appeal.'

Yashodhara dropped down to her knees and started sobbing.

The maids were taken aback. They failed to make out how such good news could make her weep. One of the maids, Kusala, who had grown close to Yashodhara, took her into her arms and said, 'It all turned out well, didn't it?'

'It's true, Kusala. It turned out to be good,' Yashodhara said. 'The warm news melted my frozen heart and it rained out in the form of tears. It's just that. Now, all of you go and make arrangements to celebrate Siddhartha's victory. One of you, run to our mother Gotami, and give her the good news. I shall go and take a bath and then meet you at the gates to welcome our master.'

When she tried to walk, she felt weak, and her feet faltered. She warded off the maidservants, who rushed to support her and walked slowly, regaining her strength with each step.

The festivities continued from evening to late night. Time after time, Suddhodana looked at his son, his eyes beaming with pride and delight.

'How was it possible? How did he stop the battle?' Gotami asked him. She wanted to know everything that had happened at the battlefield.

Suddhodana started narrating how the heroes on both sides stood at the forefront and boasted of their valour.

'I know that side of any war. Tell me first how this one was different, how my son made all the difference,' pleaded Gotami.

'Siddhartha drove to the battlefiield in his chariot. He stopped it at a distance and came on foot to stand between the two groups like a white flag.'

'Nobody knew why, but strangely for some reason, everyone suddenly fell silent as soon as he began talking. His voice sounded not only steady and serious, but humble and disciplined as well.

'He did not teach. He did not preach. He just questioned. He asked both sides the cause for their fighting. They answered like children who have no other option than to answer the questions of their teacher. When they were finished, he asked them whether the battle which they wanted to fight would remove those causes and bring excess water into the river. They said it was not possible. He asked all those who firmly believed they would neither get injured nor get killed in the battle to come forward. No one stepped forward. He said they needed water, but they would not get it even if they were wounded or killed in the battle. He asked them to think whether it was not futile to fight the battle when it would not produce what they needed. He asked them to explain why, then, they were prepared to face terrible death, destruction and sorrow. No one could explain. He told them to find out weather the weapons in their hands could be used to store the river water without wasting it. They shook their heads helplessly. He asked them to think of the best ways to share the limited water available in the river. He exhorted them to open their eyes to the fact that water gives life and people will die when there is no water. Mother river would get more emaciated to see her children fight and die to share her limited milk. He said they were free to follow their conscience. He told them that he had come there to seek answers to his questions, and as he was able to find them, he would retire. He wished that they too would retire to the delight of their parents, wives and children. Those words made them all turn homewards and leave the battlefield. They were happy that they were still alive.'

Gotami's heart flooded with boundless joy. 'My son has won,' she said gleefully and hurried to meet Siddhartha in his chambers.

One would never find an uproar or hubbub at Siddhartha's chambers. Now, when Gotami went there, she found the place silent and peaceful as usual. But then, breaking the silence, the voice of Yashodhara reached her ears as she neared Siddhartha's room and she stopped at a distance where she could make out their words.

Yashodhara was saying, 'You are capable of putting an end to war and bloodshed. We must find the way that would end war forever and bring peace and prosperity to the whole world. The aim of your exploration should be to accomplish it.'

Siddhartha laughed mysteriously.

'Whenever wars break out, people get killed on a large scale. It's true we have to put an end to them. It's not an impossible task. But, you see Yashodhara, the human mind is a bigger battlefield, where we must fight more serious battles, battles without bloodshed, but more dangerous than battles with bloodshed. There, we must fight against more dangerous and slightly more elusive enemies like ego, selfishness, prejudice, avarice, fanaticism, ignorance, superstition, love for violence and delight in killing. They make a relentless attack to enslave our hearts. Unless we win over these internal enemies, Yashodhara, winning external wars will be of no avail. We must first discover the right path that will help people overcome their prejudices.'

His words had a strong influence on her. She was able to imbibe the truth contained in them. She said, 'Yes. People are being affected by false pride, prejudice and attachment to worldly comforts. They are estranged from nobler values of life, like love and pity. These evil influences make their lives miserable. Will it ever be possible to change them? Change is inevitable. But it should lead to good, not to destruction. Nothing will be impossible if only we try sincerely.'

Gotami, who was carefully listening to them, turned pale. Her enthusiasm to go and meet them disappeared. She turned back and returned to Suddhodana, feeling weak in body and in mind. Suddhodana, who had actively participated in the celebrations of victory, was fast asleep. She didn't want to disturb him. She sat away from him and wept quietly.

Bimbanana decided to conduct a yagna. Whenever he conducted a religious ceremony, he did it with such pomp and ostentation that people talked of it till he organized another. Now, he wanted to perform a yagna that would free the members of his family and the people of his village from all kinds of diseases, and assure them of long and healthy lives.

That year, before the advent of summer, some dreadful disease had spread all over the village. People were terribly frightened as they frequently heard news of death from one family or the other. The Vedic scholars told Bimbanana that performing a special yagna was the only way to set the village free from death and disease. That yagna involved a lot of expenditure in the form of money, grain and cattle. Money was not a constraint. Bimbanana maintained his treasury well. The rich landlords of the village would gladly donate grain. The only complication was providing a large number of cattle for sacrifice. No farmer would be willing to give away his cattle. Their prosperity depended as much on their fowl and cattle as on their agricultural land. The cows supplied milk and the oxen ploughed their lands. Moreover, the animals supplied manure for the fields.

That problem always persisted. Anyone who thought of performing a yagna had to face it. The only possible solution was to take away by force the emaciated cattle that belonged to the serfs and the slaves. In fact, force was not at all needed. If the landlords asked for their cattle, the serfs and the slave would meekly give them away. They could never dare to go against the dictates of their masters. Anyone who dared would lose his life. The masters showed no pity even when the slaves pitiably begged and pleaded for their cattle. For the serfs and the slaves, yagna meant loss of property and its resultant sorrow.

Bimbanana invited Suddhodana to attend the yagna. He requested that his daughter, Yashodhara, should arrive ten days before the day of the yagna. He wished to see Siddhartha at least four days before that day, and all others on that day.

Suddhodana knew that Siddhartha was strongly against yagnas and so he did not expect him to attend it. However, he requested Gotami to send Yashodhara ten days before the ritual.

Gotami felt that it would be good for Yashodhara to visit her parents. She believed that her mother and the other women of Koliya would influence Yashodhara to take an interest in worldly affairs. She was under the impression that Siddhartha's spiritual ideas were making Yashodhara develop an aversion to sensual pleasures. It would be better for her to be away from him for some days. Her mother would understand her problem, advise her and rouse her passion for motherhood.

Gotami, who was tense about Yashodhara's relationship with Siddhartha, felt relieved. She sent for Yashodhara and, when she came, disclosed the good news. But contrary to her expectations, Yashodhara did not show excitement at the prospect of going home. On the contrary, her face turned pale, and she sat staring blankly at her mother-in-law.

'When do you wish to go?' Gotami asked, stroking her head gently.

'I shall discuss this with Siddhartha and inform you, Mother,' Yashodhara replied reluctantly.

'My son is not so unkind that he will stop his wife from visiting her parents,' Gotami said with a smile on her face.

'Kindness and unkindness are words that are often misunderstood, Mother,' Yashodhara said. 'Sometimes, we have to be unkind to people who are not kind though they may be very dear to us. Your son and I shall decide what is to be done.'

'Yashodhara, I feel that you are getting a bit too deeply involved in spiritual ideas, just like Siddhartha. I don't think it's good for you. I agree, it's very difficult to avoid his influence. But you see, Yashodhara, we are women. It is our responsibility to see that our familial relationships are well maintained. When a woman becomes dispassionate, she will lose interest in fulfilling her household duties. Life becomes intolerable and futile when we fail to attend to the duties allotted to us by nature. Men are different. They go out wandering all over the world in search of deliverance. For us deliverance is found not outdoors but within these four walls. We must urge our men – whether they be husbands, sons, kings or monks – to stay within these four walls. Our happiness, our deliverance lies herein. In human history, no woman has ever risen to fame by abandoning the shelter of these four walls. The world will look down upon such women, call them mad and punish them. I know, your mother must have told you all of this already. You mustn't forget the advice of your mother under the influence of your husband. There can be no family life for a woman without the husband. But also remember that the family is more important than the husband. A woman must try in all possible ways to save and preserve the family, even if those ways are painful to the man. You are no exception. You, too, must follow the dictates of nature.'

Gotami's voice sounded harsh but dignified. She feared that her harshness would reduce Yashodhara to tears. But Yashodhara was unmoved. There appeared no sign of realization or sorrow on her face.

'I have said what I have thought is good for you. Whether you follow it or not is left to your discretion. I have something important to attend to. Let me take my leave,' she said in a low voice.

Throughout the day, Yashodhara attended to her household work mechanically.

When Suddhodana told Siddhartha about Bimbanana's invitation, he expressed his displeasure and went to see Kalamuni. He did not return till late in the evening.

The servants lit the lamps. Yashodhara did not appear to be waiting for Siddhartha. The maidservants told Gotami that she looked grave and had been silent since morning, and that they were afraid of talking to her.

Gotami felt that her advice made Yashodhara reconsider her relationship with Siddhartha. She strongly believed that Yashodhara would mend her ways and become a normal woman in a short time. She felt peaceful. Faith would always assure peace of mind while doubt would result in restlessness. Gotami needed peace of mind.

When Siddhartha returned home, he refused to eat his meal. He drank a glass of milk, went into the garden and sat leisurely. Yashodhara had her food and joined him in the garden.

Siddhartha was singing. For the last few weeks, the two had been spending their evenings in serious discussions, which had no room for music. She sat by his side, enjoying the song. After a few minutes when he stopped, she looked at him and smiled.

'I don't think you will feel peaceful either by discussion or by music,' she said.

'When are you leaving for Koliya?' he asked.

'Perhaps tomorrow.'

'Tomorrow!' Siddhartha was surprised. 'Your father asked you to come ten days before the event, not twenty.'

'My father wanted me ten days before the yagna in the hope that I would help prepare for it.

'But I am going there now with the hope of stopping it.'

Siddhartha was stunned. It took him some time to recover.

'You want to stop the yagna? Do you think it's possible?'

'Possible or impossible – we shall know the outcome only after the attempt, not before.'

'Why do you want to make such an impetuous and bold attempt?'

'You thought it was necessary to be bold and made a bold attempt to stop the battle some days ago. The result was good for all. Now, as a daughter, I feel it necessary to try to make my father realize what is right and what is wrong. I am trying not to think about the outcome. I may succeed or end up in failure.'

Siddhartha looked at her silently for some moments and sighed.

'I too have been thinking about the futility of conducting yagnas, Yashodhara,' he said with a heavy heart. 'It is easy to stop a war, but to stop a yagna is very difficult. The hope with which a yagna is conducted depends on faith. It is done in the belief that our wishes will be fulfilled by God. Even when the wish is not fulfilled, the faith or the hope behind the faith doesn't fade away. The negative effects of war such as death and pain are common experiences for all. They can clearly be seen as the heavy price humans who wage war must pay. The result of a yagna, however, is not perceptible as it is an illusion created by the mind. It is not so easy to rid any one of illusion. Though the final result is likely to be different, illusion temporarily makes us feel safe and comfortable with the hope that our wishes will really be granted. Human beings want security from accidents, diseases, unseasonal rains, floods and famine. They do not know the honest way to shield themselves from such calamities. No one tells them about it. Until the right way is discovered, and unless they are made to walk on it, people will continue to live in illusion and perform yagnas and yagas.'

'And you see,' Yashodhara intervened, 'how they burn and waste their meagre resources for the sake of an illusory security? My father is rich. He has abundant resources in the form of money, grain and cattle. Priests and pandits come to him and instigate him to perform multiple rituals during elaborate yagnas and yagas, with the promise that it will bring him more riches, better health and God's grace. In fact, my father doesn't need any instigation. He is submerged, head deep, in such illusions. Just imagine, how much food is burnt to ashes. How many innocent animals are slaughtered at the altar! And those animals belong to the slaves, the poorest of the poor. If the grain, burnt in the name of sacrifice, is gifted away to the slaves, they will be healthy and happy. But they don't do it. All kinds of gifts are given only to the Brahmins, who anyway have everything in their favour. If the tears of the slaves are made to fall upon the sacrificial fire of the yagna, the fire will be permanently extinguished, never to burn again.' As she imagined the plight of the slaves, Yashodhara's eyes became moist with tears.

'But do you think you can put an end to all this?'

'I don't know. But I should express my thoughts at least to my parents if not to the entire world.'

'Do you think society will pay heed to the thoughts of a woman?'

'I do not know if any woman has ever tried to speak out her opinions. But I wish to know what will happen when a woman really dares to do it,' Yashodhara said decisively.

'People may think that you are voicing my thoughts,' Siddhartha said with a smile on his face.

'What is strange about it? All women do the same — follow the instructions of their husbands. But you see, my mother-in-law, today, said something very strange. I need to think deeply to understand what she meant by it. She said that a husband makes a family. But, for a wife, the family is more important than the husband.'

Siddhartha smiled again.

'Mother thought that you would save me from my strange, wild thoughts. But now she has realized that your thoughts are more dangerous than mine.'

Yashodhara and Siddhartha broke into laughter. Looking at the bright young couple, making the still night lively with their pure, pristine laughter, the stars in the sky felt shy of their lacklustre beauty and eerie silence.

―――

Bimbanana and Visista were aware of Yashodhara's attitude. They invited her to arrive ten days before, but they were prepared to feel satisfied even if she made an appearance on the day of the yagna. Yashodhara had not visited her parents even once since she went to Kapilavastu to live with her husband. Her mother, Visista, was both happy and sad about it. Whenever someone jeered at her for being happy in the absence of her daughter, she would proudly retort that she was happy to see the sprout of her stock growing up as a tree at another place.

Therefore, Bimbanana and Visista were amazed to receive Yashodhara when she arrived much before the time they expected to see her.

Which daughter will fail to remember, at the sight of her mother, that the greatest happiness for a daughter is to be in her mother's arms?

Looking at the brightness in her face, Bimbanana could tell that his daughter was much pleased with her life in Kapilavastu. He blessed her affectionately and went out to attend to his work.

Visista could not stay away from her daughter even for a moment. She showered on Yashodhara all the love and affection she had stored for her till then. She saw to it that all services were offered to her daughter unasked. It looked as if she had been granted the wish of the yagna even before it was done. Yashodhara, too, cherished deeply the simple joy of being around her mother.

The news of Yashodhara's arrival spread through the village. Women from neighbouring houses went to see her.

'What's the hurry? She will be here for a month. Why do you want to tire her when she is already tired after that long journey? Go away. You can see her after four days.' Visista sent them away.

Yet, all the familial warmth and domestic joys could not divert Yashodhara's attention from the purpose of her visit. That night, she slept peacefully and the next morning when her father was getting ready to leave the house, she went to meet him. Bimbanana thought that she wanted to ask him for something she needed.

'What do you want, my child?' he said. 'Don't hesitate to ask. This is your house. You will get whatever you need.'

'What I am going to ask you, Father, will probably cause you pain. It will probably also make you angry, but you must listen patiently.' She paused to watch her father's reaction. For a while, Bimbanana was suspicious of his son-in-law. He feared that his daughter was experiencing some inconvenience in the house of her father-in-law.

'Yasho!' he said with much concern. 'I hope Siddhartha is not indifferent to your needs. Aren't his parents kind to you?'

'No, Father! It's not that at all. I have no complaints to make against them. But I have a complaint about something here, in our house.'

Bimbanana felt confused. He couldn't understand what she was aiming at.

'What do you mean, my dear?' he said. 'What's wrong with us, here? What complaints can a daughter have against her parents!'

Yashodhara did not beat about the bush. 'Why do you want to conduct this yagna, Father?'

'Don't you know why we conduct yagnas? It's meant for the well-being of all; for the prosperity of our family, our village and all our neighbouring villages, including Kapilavastu.

This year, it has been predicted, dreadful diseases are going to spread far and wide. Epidemics and unseasonal rains are going to affect our agriculture. Sensing these disasters, our priests have advised me to conduct this yagna. It will appease the fates and ensure us of our safety. What's your doubt? Why do you want to know about the yagna?'

Yashodhara remained silent for a while before answering her father.

'It's just a matter of common sense, Father,' she said. 'Anyone who thinks a little carefully will be able to see that there is no real connection between diseases and yagnas. It is not possible to control rainfall by conducting a yagna. All the grain, all the fruits and all other kinds of food that you turn into ash in the name of yagna can instead be gifted to the poor and the needy. Isn't it a sin to waste food when hundreds of people suffer from hunger all around you? You take away cattle by force from the powerless slaves and serfs, not from the landlords. How can their silent curses cause good to you and your community? How can they believe that something good will happen to them when you sacrifice their cattle? In order to receive gifts and favours and in order to maintain their superior status in society, the Brahmin priests and scholars fill our minds with superstitious ideas in the name of religion and faith. Under their influence, we fail to understand our own follies. Do you think it is wise to burn food? Do you consider it holy to sacrifice innocent animals? Can't you open your eyes to the sufferings of the serfs? Are you blind to the hunger of the slaves? Conducting a yagna is not holy but far from it; it's a sin! For my sake, Father, please give it up.'

Bimbanana was stupefied. When he recovered, he burst out angrily. 'Did Siddhartha send you as his messenger of madness?'

'No, no. He has nothing to do with this. I have come on my own to make you give up the yagna.'

'I knew you had gone a little mad before your marriage. I thought marriage would cure you, but now I see that it has only made matters worse. Didn't your mother-in-law think of getting you treated? Or perhaps they were able to bear it as they were already used to the madness of Siddhartha.'

'Why do you call me mad, Father?' Yashodhara was a little impatient. 'Please hear me out. When I am talking reasonably, showing you reasons for the futility of the yagna, how can you call me mad? The real madness is to believe that yagnas can miraculously prevent all disasters. Death of animals and destruction of food grains can never bring about welfare. I have come here to set you free from your mad passion for yagnas.'

Bimbanana felt that it would do him no good to argue with someone who had lost her senses. Why should he talk with a madwoman even if she were his daughter? He was very angry with Siddhartha for having provoked her madness and for sending her with his message.

'Yashodhara!' he said, suppressing his anger. 'You are a woman and you should learn to be within your limits. Don't preach your nonsense before others. But I can't trust you now. A woman who dares defy her father will dare to do any other thing. Come with me.'

He held her hand tightly and took her to her bedroom. He pushed her in and locked the doors from outside. He called his wife and told her not to open the doors without taking his permission.

'What's the matter?' Visista said, aghast at the sudden harshness in her husband's voice.

'Our daughter has gone mad,' he explained. 'She was asking me to give up the yagna. I had to lock her in. Whatever she has spoken to me should not be repeated in front of anyone! Tomorrow I will send for Suddhodana and his son, and I will hand her over to them. Till then, don't allow Yasho to come out. We shall be answerable to them if she does something terrible in her fit of madness. She is stepping into affairs prohibited for women. That's sheer madness.'

Visista stared blankly at her husband, who was leaving the house. The words that Yashodhara was mad sounded to her ears like thunder.

When her husband had gone out of her sight, she opened the doors and hurried in to see her daughter.

Overcome by shame and helplessness, Yashodhara was pacing up and down the room. When she saw her mother, she burst out sobbing. Visista did not go near Yashodhara to take her into her arms but stood at a little distance. She looked a little frightened and worried. At first Yashodhara did not understand why her mother was looking at her that way. When she understood, she couldn't help pitying her mother.

'Father told you I had gone mad, didn't he?' she said weakly. 'But I want to tell you that Father is mad. That's the truth. The yagna, the animal sacrifices, the burning of food and grains, depriving the poor of their cattle – isn't it all madness? Tell me, Mother, what can we possibly gain from all this? Father thinks I am mad because I advised him to think it out before conducting the yagna. I have come home to talk to him, but he doesn't allow me to talk. He says women are not qualified to discuss such issues. You, too, are a woman, Mother.'

Visista did not expect to hear such words from Yashodhara. When Yashodhara was speaking to her, she slowly stepped backwards. As soon as she reached the doorway, she quickly jumped out, closed the doors and locked them from outside. Trembling with fear, she slumped down at the door and began to sob bitterly.

The maidservants ran to help their mistress. With their assistance, Visista reached her room. She instructed them not to enter Yashodhara's room as she was suffering from a contagious disease. They should open the doors a little, put food and water inside and shut them immediately. When the maids had left, Visista once again gave vent to her sorrow.

That night Bimbanana did his best to comfort his wife's dejected spirits. He told her that Suddhodana and Siddhartha would arrive the next morning to take Yashodhara back to Kapilavastu.

Visista, too, like her husband, felt certain that Siddhartha was responsible for their daughter's plight.

'What a noble girl my daughter used to be,' she lamented, wiping her tears. 'So tender, so beautiful, so graceful, and yet so humble; meek and gentle like a lamb. She was disciplined too, and would never go against our wishes. It's true she feared yagnas, but how enthusiastically she used to decorate the house and assist me in discharging my duties. She used to receive our guests and wait upon them so well that the guests felt jealous of me. "You have given birth to an angel," they used to say. The day after the yagna, my little darling would always fall ill, her body burning with fever. I knew it was because of the guests who had cast their evil looks on her. I used to take a handful of salt and move my hand around her face, chanting a hymn to counter the evil effect of their evil eyes. In two days, she would get well and run all over the house merrily, entertaining us all with her laughter and with her childish prattle. And now what has happened to her? How she has changed!'

There was no end to her sorrow. Lost in thought, she remained awake throughout the night.

When her mother locked the door, Yashodhara was surprised. But after some time, her sorrow and anxiety were replaced by amusement. 'What a mess they are making of it! How funny! Even my mother doesn't believe I am sane,' she said to herself and laughed.

Time and again she remembered the scene and laughed aloud. After a while, a maidservant opened the door a little to serve her meal. She was taken aback to see Yashodhara laughing by herself. Very quickly, she placed the plate of food on the floor and shut the doors again. Bimbanana, who went there just then, learnt from her what had happened. He strictly warned her that she would lose her head if she disclosed the truth about Yashodhara to anyone. The maid nodded and left the place, trembling with fear.

Yashodhara was unaware of what was going on outside her room. She now felt dejected at having failed in her mission, but she also believed that there was no use crying over spilt milk. Now she was no more interested in her parents and the yagna. She diverted her attention towards Siddhartha and she wished to be with him again.

'Nobody doubts Siddhartha's intellectual capabilities, though they do not accept his ideas,' she said to herself.

'They just think that he is on a spiritual quest. The same is the case with the Sramanas and the Charvakas. People are indifferent to their teachings, but look up to them as ideal persons, noble in thought and in action. Siddhartha could stop the battle. What would have happened if, instead of Siddhartha, I had stood between the two armies and spoken exactly those words which Siddhartha spoke to them? Surely, I would have been considered a madwoman, laughed at, or maybe even stoned to death. But why? Why is a woman's intellectual prowess mistaken for madness?

'It is only Siddhartha who considers me to be a fellow intellectual being. He values my thoughts. Others do not. For most, women have no place in the intellectual world. As long as women shut the windows of their minds and confine themselves to domestic work, they are well honoured. But the moment they open the windows, they are taken to be mad and are forced into silence. How can women win a place in society as intellectual beings? Who will let them in? Perhaps only Siddhartha can offer them refuge. But, in this regard, people will not listen even if Siddhartha tries to convince them. In order to convince people, he must have that conviction in himself first. Does he truly believe that women are capable of independent thought? After all, he has been influenced by Kalamuni and the Sramanas, who have no regard for women. Though he questions their ideas, it doesn't mean that he is completely in favour of women, and who knows, maybe he will talk in their defence.'

Yashodhara contemplated whether it was wise to depend on Siddhartha.

'First he must rise to the highest esteem in society,' she said to herself. 'He must win the hearts of all people, kings and paupers alike. That will be possible only when his spiritual quest becomes fruitful. He must find the ultimate truth which no one has discovered till now. Till then, my thoughts will continue to be seen as a madwoman's prattle. I must take care not to share my ideas with anyone but Siddhartha. Only he can pacify my intellectual unrest. He is in Kapilavastu and I must return to him at the earliest opportunity. I must set ablaze his passion for knowledge. I must make his compassion for the suffering humanity flow deep enough to submerge the whole world. I can't become a pathfinder though I have the desire to become one. So, I must make the path of the pathfinder more comfortable for him to tread upon. That shall be my aim and my life's noblest ambition.'

That realization freed Yashodhara's mind from all the misery she had undergone since that morning. For the first time in her life she experienced an inexplicable beatitude and she rested in peace.

That night, Bimbanana lay awake, worrying about his daughter. He wanted to send Yashodhara out of his house at the earliest opportunity. It was not that he did not love her. It was her unwomanly attitude that frightened something deep in him. He had already sent for Suddhodana and Siddhartha, and expected to see them the next morning.

'Will they come and take her away tomorrow?' he said to himself. 'What am I to do if they argue that she was fine when she set out for Koliya? If they say so, I shall have to blame Siddhartha for all that has happened. Everyone knows that he is averse to yagnas. They all know he mixes with the Sramanas. I can argue that my daughter has been influenced by him. So much so that she has forgotten that she is a woman and talks nonsense. But why did his madness catch my daughter and not his mother? And what is he doing? Is he leading the life of a husband with her? Or has he turned into a teacher to make her forget that she is a woman? Whatever has happened has happened. The fault lies with them and so it should be set right by them. Tomorrow, I shall demand that they take her away.' That decision freed him from his anxiety. But all was not well with him.

'What a pity!' he said to himself again. 'I never wished to see my daughter like this. Did I bring her up with so much love and affection only to see her go mad? When she was a child, I carried her on my shoulder, wherever I went. I cradled and lulled her to sleep. I wanted to give her whatever she needed. But poor soul! She never opened her mouth to ask for anything except when she asked for Siddhartha. But now, this darling of mine comes to rave at me. How unfortunate! I can't even have my lovely daughter stay with me for a few days. Here, it will be impossible to hide the truth. That maidservant is already suspicious of Yashodhara. I must get her tongue cut off. I can't bear to hear other people blame me because of my daughter. I shall have no peace of mind if the priests come to know about her madness. They will drain all my resources, forcing me to do a yagna to drive away the evil spirit that affects her.'

Without his knowledge, the truth that the priests drain the resources of people in the name of yagnas and yagas dawned upon his mind. But he was too weak at that moment to identify it and contemplate it.

That night, neither Suddhodana nor Siddhartha could get sleep. Suddhodana did not understand why he had been sent for so soon after his daughter-in-law had left for Koliya. There was cause for sending for Siddhartha. But why did they need him?

As Siddhartha was aware of Yashodhara's purpose in going to Koliya, he was not surprised by the news. But he was a little worried about the result of her visit. He knew very well that his father-in-law would never concede to give up the idea of conducting the yagna. As Yashodhara was very enthusiastic about making an attempt to stop the yagna, he had consented to her going.

Now he feared that she was in trouble. He wanted to go at once and help her out. If it was possible, he wanted to bring her back to Kapilavastu. He was too impatient to wait till it was dawn.

He remembered how the night before Yashodhara left for Koliya was spent like a minute by them. That night Yashodhara had looked very happy. It was, perhaps, because she was going to visit her parents.

'How can I stay away from you for ten days?' she said embracing him passionately.

'If you are so worried, why doesn't it appear on your face? You look very excited,' he said.

'I don't know why it's so. May be because I am going to see my mother. But really, I am sick at heart. And there seems to be a conflict, too, between the two,' she said feeling strange about her experience.

'No, I don't believe it. Come. Let me see. Let me hear.'

He held her head in his hands and looked deep into her eyes. He leant his head on her bosom and listened to her heartbeat. Yashodhara laced her hands around his neck and pulled him towards her.

Enraptured in their amorous embrace, they became insensitive to all the external world except to their own selves. They completely forgot about the next day's journey.

The thrill of becoming one resulted in them forgetting the time. Night gave way to daybreak in a moment.

But the past pleasure could not make him forget his present anxiety. Why did Bimbanana send for him and his father immediately after Yashodhara had reached Koliya? It seemed very mysterious. He lay awake the whole night thinking about it.

Suddhodana and Siddhartha were given a grand reception by Bimbanana as they were not only his guests but his relations as well. His neighbours, relatives and friends flocked to his house to meet his son-in-law who had come to Koliya after many years. They went up to him, saw him, made a few enquiries about his well-being and left happily. The process continued without interruption till it was evening.

Siddhartha offered his greetings and good wishes to all of them without getting tired or vexed. But, all the while, his eyes were searching for Yashodhara who, strangely, did not come to receive him. He was worried. He did not know why she kept herself away from him for hours after his arrival. Did her parents and the house where she was born absorb her so much that she forgot to meet him? By the time dusk gave way to darkness, the visitors returned to their houses one after another.

When they had left, Bimbanana led Suddhodana and Siddhartha to the guest house and made them sit comfortably while he remained standing in front of them. Suddhodana felt that it would be indecent for a guest to offer a seat to the host, but he couldn't help it.

Bimbanana thanked him politely and said, 'Forgive me. But you must return to Kapilavastu tomorrow along with your daughter-in-law. I am sorry to say that her mental disposition is not so good. I am sure you, too, are aware of it.'

Siddhartha sprang to his feet, casting a worried look at his father-in-law. 'Where is she? I must see her at once,' he said.

'Don't get excited, Siddhartha. You will see her,' said Bimbanana, making him sit again. 'But first, you must listen to me patiently. Yesterday she spoke to me very bitterly. She made adverse remarks regarding the yagna I am going to conduct in a few days. She talked irreverently about the noble priests and scholars. She condemned our gods and goddesses. She was ready to raise her voice against her father in defence of the slaves. Doesn't it look like madness to you? She never spoke up like that before she was married. It all must have started there in Kapilavastu. I think Siddhartha is responsible for it. You must take her away tomorrow. I shall find some excuse or other for her hasty return.'

Siddhartha became very emotional.

'Don't call her mad, Father-in-law,' he said. 'I know she has come here to make you understand the evil effects of the yagna. She wanted you to give it up for the sake of the suffering humanity. What she told you is not the result of madness but the result of her intellectual refinement. She is more refined than I in her thoughts.'

'Thoughts! For women! No, you are mistaken, my son. Women have only passions. The moment they begin to think, they go mad.'

'It's not right on your part to talk like that. I don't know about other women. Intellectual and spiritual thoughts may not do good to them. But they do a lot of good to Yashodhara. She is the rarest of the rare. What's wrong with what she has said? Like Yashodhara, I too feel that conducting yagnas is foolish. Will your gods get appeased only when the cattle of the slaves are sacrificed? Doesn't their hunger get satisfied unless food be removed from the mouths of the hungry and burnt by sacrificial fire? Don't they feel happy unless money is distributed among Brahmins during religious ceremonies? What gods are they! If gods do really exist, their compassion should be as deep and wide as the ocean. Their kindness should shower down on earth to relieve people of pain and suffering. You don't understand all this. You don't think about such outcomes at all. You call Yashodhara mad for thinking wisely about the world. You may not accept her thoughts. But all thoughts which you do not accept need not necessarily be foolish thoughts. First, take me to Yashodhara.'

Now Suddhodana could understand the real problem. He felt a little relaxed. He knew his son would be able to handle the situation gently.

'Do you mean to say that there is no God at all?' Bimbanana continued the argument.

'I do not know. What all I can say is that, if God exists, he should not be so weak as to need the assistance of Brahmin priests. Tell me. How can a weak God help us overcome serious problems?'

It was too difficult for Bimbanana to hear that there was no God. It made him tremble, as if the earth beneath his feet was giving way.

'Now I must see Yashodhara,' said Siddhartha stepping towards the door.

'Let us go,' said Bimbanana taking him to her room. 'I shall save myself not from one but from two mad people who resort to blasphemy.'

Siddhartha was anxious to meet her. When he imagined how bad she must be feeling about what had happened, he was moved to tears.

As soon as he entered the room, the door closed behind him. The room was big, but dimly lit and it took his eyes quite some time to get adjusted. When he could see, he looked for her all around, a thousand times in a moment.

In the middle of the room, there was a bed covered in white sheets. Yashodhara, dressed in thin, pink clothes, was lying on it like a garland of flowers. She was fast asleep. Her face was clear and bright. The beautiful expression on her face made him feel that she had just stopped smiling under the influence of a pleasant dream.

Siddhartha was overcome by pity and love for her.

'Yasho,' he called her softly. He sat by her and took her head on to his lap.

'You have come,' she said drowsily and embraced him.

Siddhartha forgot that he had something important to ask her, and Yashodhara forgot that she had something important to tell him. No, it wasn't forgetting. Everything was quite clear to them.

The next morning, Suddhodana and Siddhartha, along with Yashodhara, set out for Kapilavastu.

Suddhodana told Gotami all that had happened at Koliya. On her part, Gotami explained to him all that she had come to know about Yashodhara. They sat looking at each other helplessly, realizing that Siddhartha's attitude towards life had not changed even after his marriage. Instead of shaping his life, he had started to shape Yashodhara's. They thought she would give them an heir but she seemed to have developed a dislike for sensual pleasures. All their expectations, all their longings for an heir now seemed to be a mirage.

Their past fears about Siddhartha's disregard for physical pleasures and about his love of spiritual knowledge now re-entered their minds.

Gotami was in a state of uncertainty. She could not make out whether she should be angry with Yashodhara and scold her, or whether she should pity her.

All this time, she had believed that Yashodhara and Siddhartha were living like a real wife and a husband. But now, the discovery that they were only sharing spiritual experiences and possibly no carnal experiences, gave her a jolt.

Were they abstaining from physical pleasures? She wanted to know the truth, but how could she discuss such matters with them? She felt very weak at heart.

When Yashodhara went to see her, Gotami pretended to be sleeping. She was too cross to face her. Yashodhara returned feeling humiliated. She could understand that her mother-in-law was prejudiced against her, and that she now had only Siddhartha who would offer her solace.

Siddhartha remained reticent regarding Yashodhara's visit to her parents. He thought she would feel humiliated if he talked about it as she had failed to make her father give up the yagna. He behaved as if she had not gone to Koliya at all.

The journey exhausted Yashodhara, physically and mentally. It took her a couple of days to recover from the fatigue. Gotami's attitude towards her also changed in the meantime.

The third night after her return, when she was with Siddhartha, Yashodhara herself made a mention of her visit to her parents.

'My father thought that I had gone mad,' she said to Siddhartha. 'He considered everything I told him about the yagna to be sheer nonsense, the result of my hysterical frenzy.'

Siddhartha tried to comfort her by gently patting on her shoulder.

'I am not going to recall and narrate the whole incident. I just want to tell you how I look at it, and what decision I have arrived at,' she said thoughtfully.

'I have realized that our society doesn't accept women as rational human beings capable of independent, intellectual enquiry. It may take thousands of years for us women to stand on our own legs and think with our own minds. That too, only when you discover the truth about women and disclose it to the world – only when you open the gate to the path of knowledge and let women enter the arena.'

Yashodhara looked at Siddhartha, who simply nodded his head.

'From hence,' she continued, 'I have decided not to disclose my thoughts in public. We cannot go hand in hand into the public. It's of no avail. It only makes your path more difficult and delays your mission.'

Siddhartha looked at her in dismay.

'Don't delay any more,' she said. 'Break away from the bonds that prevent you from treading the path of knowledge. Find the way that will provide deliverance to the suffering humanity. Lead the world out of the darkness of dogma into the light of rational thought.'

Siddhartha sat staring at her for a while. She didn't look excited or agitated. There was a ring of sincerity in her words and a look of serenity in her eyes.

'I am also thinking about it, Yashodhara,' he said at last. 'But it doesn't seem that easy to break free from the bonds.'

'You are right. It's not at all easy. But it must happen. From today concentrate on it. I shall back you up.'

'But what about our relationship?' he asked and waited to see her reaction.

'Henceforth, its existence and non-existence should be a matter of no consequence,' she said decisively.

Siddhartha fell silent.

'Give up your concern for me,' she continued. 'Don't be alarmed about your parents. They are my responsibility. I shall protect them as my own children. It's my self-imposed duty, and I impose it on myself for my own sake.'

'Don't break your head over it, Yasho,' Siddhartha said, standing up to go. 'Be at peace.'

Yashodhara realized that it was time for him to go and sit in meditation.

When Siddhartha had left, she sat on the floor, her legs crossed in the padmasana posture. She tried to meditate but she was troubled by a multitude of wavering thoughts that swarmed across her mind. She tried hard to brush them aside but failed. Finally, she gave up meditation, lay down there on the floor itself and began to sleep. Siddhartha returned after an hour. He carefully rested her head on a pillow, lay down beside her and slept peacefully.

From that day, the lap of mother earth became their soft bed. Gotami was informed about it by the maids. She wept over it but did not question Yashodhara as to why they had resorted to such a practice.

As days passed, Siddhartha discovered that a subtle change had come over Yashodhara. In her speech and in her actions, she was more composed than before. There was more depth and seriousness in her thoughts. She looked thin as she ate little.

'She is not the same Yashodhara who met me at the temple,' he said to himself.

He realized that he too had undergone change along with her, but it did not ease his concern for her.

He tried to seek his mother's counsel about her. When he mentioned it for the first time, Gotami remained silent. But, yielding to the gentleness and concern present in his voice, she gave in when he asked her again.

'How can I understand what's going on between the two of you?' she said, taunting him a little. 'What I see and what I am informed of about you doesn't please me at all. For the change that has taken place in her, you are as much responsible as she is. It is your duty to enquire and inform us of it. We are getting older and we should not be burdened with your responsibilities. I don't know why Yasho has become so thin, and why she is so grave in her bearing. Maybe because of all the insults she had faced at her home. Your father and I have grown weak and desperate. It's up to you to deliver us and also Yashodhara from these austerities.'

Her words sounded a bit harsh and emotional to Siddhartha's ears. He could not bear it. He fell on his knees and laid his head on her feet.

As Gotami bent down and placed her hand on his head, tears welled up in her eyes and her throat was choked with emotion. When Siddhartha raised his head to see why his mother did not bless him, her tears wetted his forehead. He was deeply moved. He had never seen his mother so weak and so sorrowful. He placed his head on her feet again. 'Bless me, Mother,' he pleaded, 'let me be worthy of your upbringing and have the strength to wipe off my mother's tears.'

Gotami understood at once how deeply Siddhartha was affected by her tears. She passed her hand over his head and said, 'God bless you, my son! Have a long life!'

She made him stand up, wiped her tears and smiled at him.

'I am sorry, my son,' she said softly. 'I shouldn't have spoken to you so harshly. Take my word for it, Siddhartha, I shall talk to Yashodhara and set everything right. I am mother to her, too, and I thought a mother has the right to be angry with her daughter for a few days. I never meant to hurt you. Be happy and get a good night's sleep. Believe me, Yashodhara's heart will blossom like a lotus by tomorrow.'

Siddhartha took leave of her and went into the garden. The assurance given by his mother made him feel calm. The beautiful garden and the stillness of the night made him feel more peaceful. Somehow, an instinctive impulse of hope made him imagine that everything would be settled well between him and Yashodhara soon. He lifted his head and looked at the night sky, brightly lit with countless constellations. The stars seemed to be lighting the path that leads to the mysteries of the universe.

'How wonderfully mysterious this creation is!' he said to himself. 'The never-ending display of the sunrise and the sunset, the seasonal appearance of flowers, fruits, crops, winds and rainfall are all inexplicable mysteries. How did they come into existence? How do they continue into eternity? What gods created them? What laws guide them? Does the universe truly need a creator or does it have the potential to create itself and destroy itself? Is human life just a part of the universe and its existence, or does it have a special purpose and meaning? Why is human life ephemeral while the heavenly bodies are blessed with eternal existence? Is suffering an essential, irrevocable law of the universe or is it just the creation of human beings themselves?'

Siddhartha was so deeply engrossed in thoughts that he failed to understand the passage of time. Somewhere, far away in the east, dawn awoke with a yawn and stretched its wings to get ready to start on its flight. Suddenly it occurred to him that he had forgotten to do something important. He stood up at once and hurried toward his bedchamber..

Yashodhara was fast asleep. Her face, though a little thinner than before, looked more beautiful. The unceasing cadence of the rise and fall of her bosom made him think of the eternal rhythmic movement of the universe moving with equal pace in all directions. He sat staring endlessly at her until he fell asleep.

At daybreak, Yashodhara opened her eyes to the light of the incipient rays of the sun when, all of a sudden, she was seized by a primitive awareness of something deeply ingrained in her female conscience. Her body experienced a sweet, pleasant thrill which was unknown to it till then. Without her conscious effort, her lips widened a little to blossom into a smile. The waves of this new experience now flowed out to touch and wake up Siddhartha, who lay in deep sleep beside her.

He opened his eyes and saw Yashodhara whose eyes were concentrated on his face, but whose mind was concentrated on the knowledge of something new to her. He did not know what had happened to her, and why she looked so thrilled. Slowly he got up and sat on the bed. He did not dare to touch her.

'Yasho,' he said softly. 'What is the matter?'

Yashodhara smiled sweetly.

'The work of creation has been accomplished,' she said.

Before he could understand what she meant by it, she laid her head on his lap, looked deep into his eyes and smiled.

Siddhartha was perplexed. He was utterly devoid of all thought and all feeling. His body failed to react to her touch as it used to react till then.

Yashodhara understood that he did not respond to her. She patted his cheeks to bring him out of his stupor.

'I am in ecstasy,' she said. 'Won't you share my joy?'

Siddhartha looked into her eyes once and bent his head down.

'You should not be like the ascetics who negate life without experiencing the joys and sorrows of life. When they are afraid of bonds and keep away from them, how can they break them? You must see, you must taste and feel all that is perceptible to the senses. Then, when you break away from them, your real mettle comes to light. The world will see and recognize it. You will experience it. I need not tell you. You know it better,' she said.

Siddhartha lifted his head, looked at her and smiled. Once again Yashodhara was thrilled.

The fresh, bright morning was also thrilled to see the young couple affectionately embrace each other.

Yashodhara attended to her usual household duties. When they were finished, she bathed, got dressed, carefully adorned herself with flowers and then she went to see her mother-in-law.

Gotami had spent a sleepless night as she was deeply anxious about Yashodhara. In the morning, even when she was at work, she did not cease to think about her. When she was in such a confused state of mind, all of a sudden Yashodhara delighted her eyes like a fresh, well-blossomed lotus flower.

Her delight reached its peak when Yashodhara confidently confided to her: 'Mother, I am pregnant. I have taken up the work of moulding a child in my womb.'

The next moment Yashodhara was in Gotami's arms. All the pent-up sorrow in Gotami's heart melted at the warmth of her delight and flowed out of her eyes, drenching both of them. 'My child,' she said. 'What a fool I was to misunderstand you! You are our goddess, come to deliver us. I can't explain how much our family is indebted to you. Forgive me, daughter, oh! Forgive me.' In a frenzied state of happiness, she failed to understand what she was uttering.

The news spread at lightning speed. For the last several months, Suddhodana had confined himself to his house. He neither went out to see people nor received guests at home. He looked dull and uninterested, lost in pensive thought. The news of an heir suddenly energized his body and activated his mind. In a minute, he was all over the village disclosing the news and giving away gifts.

The whole village went on a jubilant celebration, but Siddhartha kept himself away from it. He remained alone the whole day. He did not go even to see his parents.

Everyone felt that time was moving fast. In no time, days passed into weeks, and weeks passed into months.

Day and night, Gotami cared for Yashodhara as she would care for herself. Day by day, Siddhartha was spending much of his time all alone in deep thought. Yashodhara was gaining weight. She looked healthy and happy. Siddhartha was emaciated and serious. One day, Yashodhara requested

Gotami to allow her to spend a little more time with Siddhartha.

'I didn't mean to separate you from my son,' Gotami said regretfully. 'I always keep you company only to ensure that Siddhartha will not make you and your son become averse to worldly pleasures with his dispassionate teachings.'

Yashodhara laughed heartily. Gotami could not make out its meaning. She left the room, providing privacy to the couple.

As soon as they were left to themselves, Siddhartha poured out in an unending stream all the thoughts locked up in his heart.

'You have been enjoying your life in the company of your mother-in-law,' he said. 'It has given me much time and freedom to go about visiting people and places. It pains me to disturb you when you are supposed to be peaceful, but I can't help it. Wherever I go, I see only pain and suffering. It seems to me that the entire humankind is submerged in a sea of sorrow. For the multitude of the poor, even the birth of a child is no cause for joy. Dreadful diseases have become rampant. When unattended to, even minor illnesses lead to death. The old are left uncared for and unprovided for. All these are related to physical suffering. In matters of the spirit, it is not surprising that the situation is worse. People are totally bereft of nobler feelings like love, pity and mercy. Jealousy, hatred, cruelty and a passion for war have taken deep root in the human heart. Nobody sees that they are getting strongly addicted to an unending chain of baser feelings. Everyone talks of deliverance without understanding how deliverance is strongly connected with love and compassion. Are physical needs superior to spiritual needs, or the other way around? I fail to understand. More serious than these is the problem of caste. How can we consider a person to be either superior or inferior to the other by virtue of the person's birth into a particular family? People who are fortunate to be born into wealthy and well-educated, noble-caste families do not use their privileges for the upliftment of the meek and the weak. Instead, they use their power to oppress the ill-fated. I am much distressed. I wish to seclude myself from this sinuous society. But the woes of such helpless people dissipate my distress and drive me to find a way for their deliverance.'

Yashodhara absorbed his words just as the scorched earth absorbs the first fresh showers of rain after the severe summer.

'I can't adjust myself to the ways of this shallow society,' he continued. 'I feel averse to all physical pleasures of the world. It's only you who ties me down to this house, and when the child is born, it also may tie me down with a stronger knot.'

Yashodhara remained silent for some time, and then she looked at Siddhartha decisively. 'You think deeply about human sorrow. It means that you have developed a very strong bond with humanity. Treat me and our son as part of humankind, and then these bonds will naturally disappear.'

Siddhartha's eyes were filled with gratitude and he nodded his head.

In the evening, whenever Siddhartha went to visit Kalamuni or some of the Sramanas, Yashodhara spent her time cleaning Siddhartha's and her own belongings. She liked to clean with her own hands all those places where she would sit with Siddhartha, engaged in affectionate, personal conversation, or in serious philosophical discussions.

She did her work, recalling her conversation with Siddhartha, with all the seriousness of a girl memorizing her lessons. Gotami tried to prevent her from doing such menial work, but Yashodhara considered it a pleasure. She would complete that work by dusk, light the lamps and wait for Siddhartha like the clear sky waiting to be flooded by the moonlight.

On that day too, Yashodhara was seriously involved in her work when the buzz of a crowd coming from Gotami's apartment distracted her attention. She left her work and hastened to find out what it was. She saw a small crowd of neighbouring women standing in Gotami's room, talking insensitively to her. Just when she entered the crowd, the buzz subsided and a clear, deep voice was heard saying loudly, 'We have borne this nonsense for long.'

Some of the maidservants tried to silence her, but the woman continued to speak, turning a deaf ear to them.

'When others complained of it, we thought they were spreading rumours,' she said. 'But today, we saw it ourselves. It was the unholiest of all unholy acts. Do you know what horrible crime your son has committed? How dare he carry a wretched untouchable all the way to his house in the outcastes' colony and attend to his filthy illness! What ablutions can cleanse his sinful hands? How can we live in peace as your neighbours? How can we protect our children from the evil influence of your son?'

Yashodhara could understand what the commotion was about. Siddhartha helped a person who was suffering from some illness to reach his home. That person belonged to an untouchable caste.

As there was no danger of a physical assault on her mother-in-law, she felt relieved. But, the next moment when she thought about the noble work accomplished by Siddhartha, her heart brimmed over with pride. A deep sense of satisfaction filled her eyes with tears of joy. Very quickly she made her way through the crowd and stood in front of Gotami as a shield of defence.

The crowd was taken aback by the sudden appearance of Yashodhara and her defensive posture. Its commotion subsided.

Yashodhara raised her hands up above her head and joined her palms as a token of greeting.

'I request you all to return to your homes,' she said with great composure. 'You bawled out your dissatisfaction at what Siddhartha had done. You know that Prajapati Gotami has nothing to do with what he has done. You also know that you will not get an answer from her. But, in spite of it, you have come here. You know very well, and I know, too, why you demand her to answer for Siddhartha. If you ask Siddhartha, he will give an answer which none of you can refute, and which cannot be questioned back. I know very well that you don't need answers. Your restlessness cannot be appeased with answers. What you need is a rethinking of your own traditions and prejudices. No one should deviate from what you think is a well-trodden path. Even when the old path becomes impassable, you don't want anyone to lay down a better, new path.'

Yashodhara paused a little and then continued.

'I honour you all as I honour my mother. Believe me, Siddhartha is just trying to lay down a new path. Remember, the path you walk upon was once newly laid by someone. I do not know what the people, who laid the new path, did to overcome the dissent of the people who wanted to follow the older path. To make you take to his path, Siddhartha would never resort to violence; nor would he resort to make false promises and allure you. Don't be worried about your children. Those people whom we consider outcastes are human beings, exactly like us. You believe that the creator has ordained our lives to be noble and theirs to be ignoble. No. It's not that way. It's not the creator but we, the fortunate, who stamp them as ignoble and make them struggle for their survival. It is easy to take one's life. Siddhartha is not at all interested in it. He wants to protect life as he considers it precious. He wants to set humanity free from all kinds of suffering. You cannot prove his work to be evil. If any one of you can prove it, go to Siddhartha. Go, try it.'

The crowd was astonished by the eloquence of Yashodhara. It was not an angry outburst of emotion. It was a cool, thoughtful, yet provocative, address. They had never seen in their lives, till then, a woman stand before a crowd and address them so boldly. It was, perhaps, for that reason that they did not react as they would have usually. They did not heckle her, nor did they curse her. Overpowered by her eloquence and reasoning, they simply left the place.

Gotami could not believe it. She felt it was just a dream. She had no inclination to congratulate Yashodhara. She knew that Yashodhara was deeply inspired by the ideas of Siddhartha. She also knew that she was influencing him to do something. But she could not digest those facts when they appeared so clearly before her eyes.

This was not the first time she had received complaints against Siddhartha. He would do something unusual or something out of the way. The neighbours would come complaining about it. She would pacify them saying that they should take it easy as he was a child. Never did she stand so strongly in his defence as Yashodhara did now.

Was Yashodhara the real strength behind Siddhartha? Or, having received strength from him, was she using it to strengthen him more? To what misfortune would it all lead!

Yashodhara turned around and stood facing her mother-in-law. She could see that Gotami had not yet recovered from her distressed mood.

'Don't be worried,' she said cheerfully. 'Everything will be fine for him. He has saved a life, hasn't killed anyone. You know well that saving life is always good. One who does good is always blessed. If you understand this, you will have no occasion for worrying.'

She made Gotami lie down on the bed and stood fanning her for some time. When Gotami fell asleep, she opened all the windows, went out and closed the door after her.

That night it was very late when Siddhartha reached home. Yashodhara did not talk to him. Quietly, she made arrangements for his supper. He was uninterested in eating a sumptuous supper. Having eaten a few fruits, he sat down in meditation. As usual, Yashodhara sat in front of him and started to meditate. They sat still, their eyes unconsciously shedding tears, till it was time for daybreak.

When they opened their eyes to the chirping of the birds in the garden, Yashodhara broke the ice.

'We know, the two of us, what had happened. You need not explain it to me. Go to bed. Rest a while,' she said softly.

Siddhartha sighed wearily.

'Henceforth, the word rest will not rest in my mind, Yashodhara,' he said. 'Anyone who sees the horrible scene I have seen can never rest in peace. You can't imagine how poverty and disease make a joint attack on the wretchedly poor. They don't look like human beings, alive with flesh and blood, but like living skeletons waiting for death. They exist plainly, leaving everything to the will of a god who no one knows really exists or not. I wish to set aside my quest for true knowledge and spend the rest of my life in their service. Tell me, Yasho. Is it right to seclude myself from the suffering humanity and go in search of something which I am not sure of attaining?'

Yashodhara could understand and feel the severity of the clash of opinions, and its resultant uncertainty and vexation, going on in Siddhartha's mind.

She wanted to set him free from his uncertainty. She did not wish that he should move away from the course of action she had set out for him.

'Service to humanity is a noble work. I don't doubt it,' she said. 'But even when you spend all your life in it, human misery will continue to exist. Unless the root is unrooted—'

'Yes,' Siddhartha agreed. 'I too thought the root must be discovered, and so I returned home. Otherwise, I would have stayed on in the colony of the wretched for ever. This house and these pleasures do not delight me any more. I abhor them all and I feel compelled to give them up.'

Yashodhara felt a deep sense of satisfaction as the aim of her life seemed to be at the brink of fulfilment. She laid her head at his feet.

As Siddhartha passed his hand over her head, his love for her, now mixed with gratitude, passed through the tips of his delicate fingers, travelling deep into her heart.

'I will leave, Yasho, only after I see the child,' he whispered in her ears.

Yashodhara experienced the bliss of beatitude.

Two months later, Gotami thought that she should show more concern for Siddhartha than for Yashodhara. She felt guilty at heart for having neglected her son in the fond expectation of a grandson. Of late, Siddhartha spent much of his time wandering all over the village as well as visiting the neighbouring villages. He was hardly seen at home. Though he looked emaciated from all the wanderings, his face was bright and peaceful.

'Why do you go about wandering, Siddhartha? See, how thin and weak you have become,' Gotami said passing her hand over his body.

The next moment she withdrew her hand feeling a little shocked. She was sure that his body failed to react to her touch. She felt that he was not her son but a stranger who looked like her son.

'What happened to you, my son?' she said, her voice trembling with anxiety. 'What's going on inside you? Do you see me? Do you hear me? Don't you feel the touch of your dear mother?'

'I do not know why, Mother,' he said. 'These days, I seem to be moving away from all bonds.'

'But why! Why doesn't your mother's touch affect your heart?' Gotami's voice sounded feeble with sorrow.

'It is to set you free from the sorrow that I hear in your voice, Mother,' he said. 'I am moving away from all of you, and in the coming days, I shall cease to be your son for ever. Set free from these palaces and these people, I wish to know who I really am.'

'You want to know! Don't you know who you are? You are the son of Suddhodana. The one to whom Mahamaya Devi gave birth. The one dearly brought up by Mahaprajapati Gotami. You are Yashodhara's husband. Father of the child she bears in her womb. The heir to all the wealth of your father. What more do you want to know, my child?' Gotami began to sob.

'I want to discover what I will be like when I get rid of all these attributes. If I still have an existence, what will be its purpose, its meaning and its goal? To find answers to these questions, I need to leave this house.'

Like a man walking in sleep, Siddhartha moved away from his mother, unaffected by her sobs of sorrow; and Gotami slumped down to the floor.

One night, Yashodhara laid Siddhartha's hand on her womb. Siddhartha felt the child moving slowly inside Yashodhara like a small fish plodding along the waters of a pond. He felt a tinge of delight.

At once Siddhartha withdrew his hand as if he had received a sudden shock. His body trembled all over..

'I thought my dispassion for the world was as full as the full moon. I fear now the birth of the child is going to eclipse it,' he said sadly.

'It doesn't matter,' said Yashodhara. 'An eclipse will last a little while only. Then, the moon will flood the dark sky with his bright light.'

'If that is true, let's call the child Rahul if it is male. Let me see how many hours I need to free myself from the shadow of desire he casts on me,' Siddhartha said, wrinkling his brow.

'Mahamaya took seven days to part from you. Can't you give your child that much time to make him feel the pleasure of your company before you part.'

Siddhartha took her hand into his as if he were making a promise. 'Your touch is different from what it used to be,' she said.

'Yes, it's not the same. It won't be. Don't be depressed.'

Siddhartha meant to comfort her, but Yashodhara interrupted him with a sweet smile. 'This is not the occasion for me to get depressed. I feel glad and proud.'

'How can I repay your cooperation?'

His words failed to express the intensity of gratitude he felt for her.

'Do I have a cause, a selfish motive behind it? Maybe I do. Or maybe I don't. Forget about repayment, Siddhartha. I wish you to do something for me. No, it isn't a wish. It is an order to be carried out by you.'

Yashodhara was excited.

'An order! What's that?' Siddhartha was surprised. He wanted to know at once what it was.

'Have patience. I shall disclose it when time demands that I do so.' Yashodhara smiled at him.

Yashodhara gave birth to a male child. Siddhartha was not at home then. When the news reached him, he hurried home anxiously.

Gotami did not allow him to see Yashodhara as she was very tired and weak. Instead, she brought the child and put him in his father's hands.

Siddhartha looked at the child, his eyes filled with wonder and amazement. He could understand that the touch of the child allured him strongly. In order to neutralize it and feel as he would feel at any other person's touch, he thought he would really need seven days. If he experienced it longer than that, he would get strongly attached to it, and then, it would be too difficult for him to break away from it. How clever Yashodhara was to have foreseen it all!

That night, Siddhartha pondered at length about the bonds that bind human life. Even when he thought he had freed himself from all passions, the touch of the child had its alluring impact on him. He tried to understand the purpose and meaning of all attachments and their resultant joys and sorrows that came naturally by birth. He tried to estimate the strength of attachment with which his parents were bound to him. He understood why they would feel deep sorrow and pain if he abandoned them. He reviewed how, different from all other women in the world, Yashodhara could set him free from their relationship. Did she simply follow the advice he had given her before they got married? Or did she free him because she too, like him, was deeply involved in the philosophical investigation of the world? Whatever it might be, he was quite certain that

Yashodhara was a very rare woman – so different and so distinct.

His thoughts made him strongly believe that his way had been cleared. He wanted to set himself on the path of a person who was immune to all worldly pleasures and social relationships so that he would be able to discover the hidden secret of sorrow. That should be the only desire to bind him to the world. His body should be the place for his experiment. His wisdom should be his guide. No one else would be able to help him reach his goal.

One day he told Yashodhara about it.

'All people who seek deliverance think only of their personal deliverance. You are the first to think about the deliverance of humankind. So you are your own teacher and your own disciple,' she said.

Siddhartha wondered how deeply she was involved in his investigation.

He thought for a while what he should do if the results of his experiment would be useful to him alone. But the next moment he struck off such doubts as meaningless. Whatever might be the result of his experiment, it must be conducted.

He sat in the garden, lost in deep thought, till daybreak. Then, he went in. He had a bath, dressed himself and went to see his wife. Yashodhara was suckling the baby. He thanked her profusely for allowing him to view the most wonderful scene of motherly affection.

Yashodhara smiled at him.

'Mere gratitude will not suffice. You must follow my orders,' she said.

'Sure,' he said. 'But if you ask me to find it out myself, it will never be possible for me.'

He laughed, expressing his helplessness.

'I shall let you know now itself,' she said.

Rahul had fallen asleep. She moved him aside a little and sat upon the bed. Siddhartha sat attentively facing her.

'Don't ask me why I wish to give this command. If you can understand it, it's all right. Otherwise, don't think too seriously to know why I commanded you to do so. You are going to sever all your bonds and leave the house on the fifth day after this. When you have left, Yashodhara should be wiped off completely from your memory. You should never mention my name, my thoughts and my consent for your going away. It should all be confined to us.'

Siddhartha nodded his head.

Yashodhara could see that he understood what she meant by it.

'You know well what kind of importance is given to women in our society. It is impossible for a woman to break away from all bonds and go in search of the truth. But, when you have discovered the way for the deliverance of humankind, leave that path open to women too. Only then it will be possible for women to get liberated.'

'How can I say now that my path will be useful to all, including women?'

'When the true path is discovered, you will know whether it is useful for all or not.

'Then, think of women. For these five days, we three shall live together. On the fifth, when you leave, you need not seek my consent again. Whenever your feet wish to walk into the wide, open world, you are free to go.'

Siddhartha pushed back the soft hair that covered Rahul's forehead, kissed it gently and left.

Siddhartha was leaving the house.

There was no one who could comfort Suddhodana and Gotami, who were in bitter grief.

Yashodhara was fast asleep with Rahul by her side.

She never knew that Siddhartha had paid them a visit before he left.

For four months, a group of Buddhist monks had been camping in the woods on the outskirts of a village, peacefully attending to their work. When the people of the village heard that four female monks were going to join the group in a few days, they made all the necessary arrangements for their stay.

The woods looked lovely with tall, green trees and all kinds of flowering plants. A mountain stream was flowing just beside the camp. The fresh waters of the stream refreshed the hearts of the monks to make them feel more peaceful. Every day, at noon, they went through the village asking for alms. People happily offered them a little part of whatever food they had cooked for themselves. The monks engaged themselves in meditation and in discussions over spiritual questions. In the evenings, they taught people the Buddhist dharmas.

For a few days after her arrival, Yashodhara examined carefully the village and its people. She could clearly see that it was a prosperous village. The land was fertile, and there was sufficient water throughout the year. The people appeared to be living in peace and happiness. Outwardly, everything appeared to be quite satisfactory, but there was something alarming about the life of the people. In four days, Yasho could find out what it was. It was related to their moral and spiritual values.

All the rich upper-caste people in the village were conceited and pedantic. There was an air of arrogance in whatever they said and in whatever they did.

They were generous enough to offer alms to the monks. They did it not out of love and respect for the monks but to vie with each other and display their wealth. They proudly boasted of their own achievements and jealously condemned those of others. They pampered their sons and repented when they turned out to be haughty and uncaring towards their own parents. They were jealous of the riches of their own kith and kin, and showed envious resentment for the possessions of their neighbours. In short, their morality and spirituality were just an outward show, aimed at concealing their hypocrisy. Regarding their treatment of the serfs and slaves, they were all alike. They considered them to be inhuman beings born to do society's mean and dirty work.

Yashodhara was extremely sorry for those people whose lives were devoid of love and pity.

'Can we stay here for four months? Do you think we can change these people?' she said to Kusala, her companion and fellow female monk.

'You can do it,' said Kusala, confidently.

Kusala was right for she had seen in the past how Yasho could influence people into giving up their corrupt ways of life and follow the path laid by the Buddha.

Her soothing words of advice touched the hearts of people who listened to her. The services she had rendered to the diseased saved them from the jaws of death and made them lead a new, meaningful life.

Both Yasho and Kusala used to spend their daytime catering to the needs of the sick and the helpless old people of the villages they visited. In the evenings, Yashodhara taught the people who came to her the eight-fold path of the Buddha. People listened to her with grave attention as she gently explained to them in a sonorous voice the righteous ways of living proposed by the Buddha.

The same thing was happening there in that village too. But, ten days after their arrival, a dreadful, contagious disease broke out in the village. The streets where the rich lived were the first to be affected by it. Four people died in a couple of days. People trembled with fear and turned to the monks for help.

The monks were indecisive about their course of action. The severity of the disease frightened them as well. Most of them felt that it was unnecessary to risk their lives. Yasho did not agree with them.

'Aren't we morally bound to these people who have given us shelter and alms for the last four months? Is it proper to desert them when they need our help the most? This is not the course of action set to us by the Buddha.'

Yashodhara tried to convince the monks of their duty.

'Service to humanity doesn't mean we should endanger our own lives in the process. When the inevitability of death glares at us, isn't it wise on our part to step out of its course?' said one of the monks.

'It's true. To be alive is very important. But more important is to save the lives of people,' Yashodhara said softly.

'I agree with you,' said another monk. 'But, in this case, since we are not sure of saving them from death, won't it be foolish to sacrifice our own lives?'

'Haven't we already sacrificed all that we had? For what purpose? Isn't it for the sake of removing sorrow from the world? Now we have nothing more left to sacrifice except our own lives. To save our lives shall we give up the noblest work of service to humanity – the greatest dharma taught to us by the Buddha? Giving up that dharma only means giving up our faith in the Buddha.'

The monks felt ashamed of themselves. They stood silently with their heads bent down.

'Those who are afraid of death are free to leave the camp immediately. Only those who wish to seek peace and deliverance by serving the helpless people of this village should stay here. I don't wish to compel you to do anything against your wishes,' Yashodhara spoke without getting excited or emotional.

The monks dispersed, discussing the issue among themselves. The next morning one third of the monks left the camp.

With the remaining monks, Yashodhara and Kusala started attending to the needs of the sick. They gave them whatever medicines were available for that disease, fed them at regular intervals, cleaned their bodies, and washed their clothes.

The monks took every care to see that they themselves would not be attacked by the disease. It was not because they were afraid of it, but because there would be no one to treat the people if they too fell ill. The work was very hard and sometimes very unpleasant, requiring them to clean the excrements of the patients. Not even one's own children would like to do such work.

In about a month and a half, the terrible disease surrendered to the indomitable will of Yashodhara and her team.

When the conditions in the village became normal again, the people tried to deify Yashodhara, but she gently prevented them from doing so. She requested the elders of the village to do justice to the unfortunate sections of that village if they truly wanted to pay back the services of the monks.

The debts of the serfs were written off. The slaves were emancipated. Wealth was evenly distributed among all people. As castes and classes were annihilated, the entire population of the village stood on equal footing.

They all accepted the Buddhist dharma. The elderly people joined the sangha and became monks.

Towards the end of the month of Chaitra, the first month of the year, Yashodhara fell seriously ill. She knew it wasn't an ordinary illness. She told everyone that she needed to sit in solitary meditation for four days and confined herself to her room. Only Kusala entered the room to serve her the usual meals.

Yashodhara tried to bear the pain caused by the illness with as much ease as possible. She spent much of her time in meditation and the rest of her time in recalling to her mind the memories of her past life.

Those memories were precious to her. They made her forget her pain temporarily. Sweet memories of the distant past eclipsed the severe physical pain of the present, but sprouted a new sweet pain in her heart. She spent her time helplessly swaying from memories to pain and from pain to memories.

On the fifth day, early in the morning, Kusala entered the room with a glass of milk.

Her heart throbbed with fear as she looked at Yashodhara.

Yashodhara looked at Kusala with a feeble smile on her lips. She waved her hand, requesting Kusala to help her get up from bed. With great difficulty, she sat down on the floor to go into meditation.

'Kusa,' she said.

Her voice sounded feeble. Her lips trembled as she gathered up all her strength and spoke, 'I am seventy-eight years old now. An appropriate age to respond to the call of death. Don't feel sad. Send word to those who should know.'

Slowly and softly, she closed her eyes and her lips, never to open them again.

Kusala stood still like a stone, unable to move out of the room and tell others what had happened. Since Siddhartha left Yashodhara, she had lived in close association with her. Now, as that association was suddenly cut off, it was impossible for her to accept the truth. The memories of all the important incidents that involved Yashodhara rushed into her mind, coming alive again.

She remembered very clearly that night when Siddhartha left his home. The entire house was in a pell-mell, but Yashodhara did not even come out of her room. Kusala had then thought that perhaps Yashodhara was not aware of Siddhartha's departure. She ran at full speed to inform her about it. But, when she found Yashodhara fast asleep on her bed with her son beside her, she was shocked. She doubted for a while whether Yashodhara knew what was happening in the house. She decided to wait till Yashodhara woke up from her sleep and then inform her that Siddhartha had left.

An hour before daybreak, Yashodhara woke up as the child wetted the bed and started crying. She got up, changed the bedclothes and lay down again, suckling the child.

Kusala could not remain silent any longer.

'Madam, something terrible has happened,' she said, her voice faltering with sorrow.

Yashodhara looked at her peacefully.

'You mean to say that Siddhartha Gautama has left the house, don't you?'

Kusala was astonished. She couldn't digest the fact that Yashodhara was able to sleep so peacefully knowing well that Siddhartha was going to desert her.

'Yes, madam,' she said. 'My master, Suddhodana, and my mistress, Mahaprajapati Gotami, are wild with grief. They have been crying bitterly and no one has been able to comfort them, not even their son, Ananda.'

'Their grief is too deep to be comforted by human words. Only time has the power to mitigate the intensity of such deep wounds.'

'Madam, why don't you go and try to console them? Please, try once. I shall look after the child,' Kusala pleaded.

'Their sorrow will only enhance if they set their eyes on me. It's of no use, Kusala. Better you go and watch them carefully and inform me about their condition from time to time.'

Kusala nodded her head and left to follow the instructions. When she went to Gotami's quarters, even from a distance, she could hear Gotami crying loudly and bitterly. She went and stood aside at the threshold, silently watching the distress of her mistress. It was only after some time that

Gotami felt Kusala's presence. And the next moment, she looked fierce. Her face turned red with anger, and her eyes were wild with frustration.

'Is your mistress sleeping peacefully?' she shouted angrily. 'She has forsaken my son now as she has her own son to gloat over. Can you find such an unkind woman anywhere in the world? Did she send you with her eyes to watch gleefully how I lament the loss of my son? Can't she spare a moment to console her mother's ailing heart? Was she born into this world only to deprive us of our son?'

Gotami could speak no more. Her voice choked up. She sat on her bed, sobbing endlessly.

Kusala had neither the intimacy nor the courage to console her mistress. Wiping her tears, she turned back to go to Yashodhara. By the time she went, the sun had already climbed up the sky. Yashodhara was busy dressing up Rahul after giving him a bath. Kusala helped her silently for some time and then, unable to control herself, informed her what she had heard at Gotami's quarters.

'Your mother-in-law is sore at you. She blames you for all that has happened.'

'If blaming me alleviates her sorrow, let her do it, Kusala,' Yashodhara said. 'We should take the censure of our well-wishers as their blessings to us. I know how much she loves me and you have seen for yourself how badly she is affected as Siddhartha has abandoned her. After a few days, I shall take Rahul to her and put him in her lap. If she takes him tenderly into her arms as she had taken Siddhartha when he was a newborn child, it means that she will forgive me and overcome her grief over time.'

Kusala was greatly surprised. She could not understand how Yashodhara could remain so calm and composed even after being deserted by her husband.

'Your mother-in-law was sore because you do not cry at the loss of your husband,' she said, plucking up her courage.

Yashodhara patted Kusala on her shoulder. The maid looked into her mistress's eyes once, and bent down her head, unable to bear the pity and the kindness expressed through them.

'Don't think much about it, Kusala,' Yashodhara said. 'From today you, too, must sit in meditation along with me. It will relax you and offer you peace of mind. Don't say it will be impossible for you. It will be very easy for anyone to meditate provided one makes up one's mind to undertake it. Now look after my son for some time. I want to attend to my personal work.'

Yashodhara handed over Rahul to Kusala and left.

———

Kusala remembered all the struggles and anxious moments that Yashodhara faced in the first few months after Siddhartha left, and how courageously and nobly she bore them all. She couldn't help appreciating her fortitude. On that day when Yashodhara took her son, Rahul, to Gotami, Kusala felt terribly weak at heart. The other maidservants told her every day about the bitter comments Gotami would make against Yashodhara. She kept them to herself and never disclosed them to Yashodhara. She knew very well that her mistress had no patience to listen to such things.

Yashodhara bathed the child, dressed him in new clothes and said, 'Come, let's go and put Rahul in the hands of my mother-in-law.'

'Madam, do you think she will accept the child?' she said doubtfully.

'It's all right. Follow me,' Yashodhara said confidently.

Kusala had no other choice than to follow Yashodhara. As they neared Gotami's apartment, Yashodhara examined everything carefully, paying attention even to minute details. The rooms looked untidy. Gotami looked unkempt. It was clear that she was not eating well and not sleeping well. Constant weeping had turned her eyes dry and red. Like uncleaned dirt, her sorrow was piling up in her heart, waiting for someone to come and clean it up.

She was sitting on the floor in a corner of the room, staring blankly at a portrait of Siddhartha that hung on the wall.

Yashodhara moved up to her in a slow, dignified gait as if she had come to cleanse her heart of sorrow, and gently placed the child in her lap.

Gotami turned her stare from the portrait of Siddhartha to the child in her lap. For a while she seemed to be uninterested.

Rahul, the child, moved his tender limbs, hitting and kicking Gotami as if he wanted to awaken her dead spirits. He tried hard to put his tiny fist into his mouth, failed in his attempt and smiled, exposing his bare, toothless mouth.

Gotami could resist no more. She lifted the child and pressed him to her bosom. Yashodhara sighed in relief.

Tears ran down Gotami's face, wetting Rahul's thin hair. Yashodhara asked two maidservants to clean the rooms and the courtyard and supervised the work. She told Kusala to go into the garden and gather the flowers that had fallen to the ground.

Gotami moved out of the room when the work commenced. She did not want to expose Rahul to dust. She returned after an hour as the child began to cry, unable to control his hunger.

'Take him. He is hungry,' she said, handing Rahul to Yashodhara. Yashodhara took the child and started suckling him. Gotami sat beside Yashodhara and fondly watched the child satisfy his hunger. After some time, Rahul fell asleep and the two women stood up.

Yashodhara handed Rahul to Gotami. She bent down and touched Gotami's feet to seek her blessings.

'You know everything about your son, Siddhartha,' she said, trying to start the impending conversation with Gotami.

'You must stop grieving for him. I have heard people say that the grief of a mother will have an adverse effect on whatever her son wishes to achieve. Bless your son so that he succeeds in reaching his goal. My son needs your love and I need your experience in bringing him up. Your son has great faith in you. It was for that reason he could leave his home without anxiety for his son. He was confident that you would bring up his son just as you had brought him up after the death of Mahamaya. He will not expect, even in his dreams, that you will fail to fulfil his hopes. Look at his son in your hands and forget the past.'

Gotami held Rahul in one hand and affectionately put the other around Yashodhara's shoulders. The eyes of both the women were filled with tears. They were not tears of sorrow, nor of joy, but tears of a feeling more sublime than joy and sorrow.

Kusala admired the patience with which Yashodhara could bring back into the house the peace and happiness that were lost to it for several days. From that day, she followed Yashodhara and did whatever she was told to do with unflinching faith in her.

Yashodhara taught Kusala how to meditate and Kusala learnt it attentively.

Rahul was growing up. Now, he was looking at people and recognizing their faces and voices. Now, his meaningless cries were slowly changing into meaningful words and he was beginning to address people and to delight them with his childish prattle. Now, he was trying to stand on his own and move a step or two forward and tumble over. Now, as his teeth were beginning to appear, he was grinning more often to expose them.

Gotami was carefully watching him and enjoying everything he said and did.

Yashodhara was feeling greatly relieved.

When Rahul gave up sucking milk from her breast, she started eating very little and spent much of her time all alone in meditation. Everyone could understand that she preferred to be silent by herself.

Kusala could discern some mysterious change coming over Yashodhara. Her face was radiant. Endless love and kindness emanated from her eyes. Sometimes she could see that there was an indiscernible expression on her face, as if she longed to see someone.

Was she expecting to see Siddhartha again? Did she want him to come back to Kapilavastu to see her?

Time and tide wait for none. Seasons were setting in and setting out. Suddhodana and Gotami were growing old. Rahul was seven years old, and it was time he started learning his lessons.

But Yashodhara was not very concerned with those developments; she was always found deeply immersed in her meditation.

And sometimes she could be found staring ahead of her, as if she were in a trance. She would be found staring – ceaselessly and patiently waiting for something. Her eyes were reaching beyond the green fields of Kapilavastu, beyond the hills that stretched to the south of Kapilavastu. She was staring at the far-off unknown places that filled her imagination, looking for something that she sweetly cherished deep down in the core of her heart.

Anyone who saw her in that state could tell that people and things at home and in Kapilavastu had lost their meaning for Yashodhara. She was untouched and unmoved by anything. Neither personal nor public affairs could influence her benumbed heart.

Gotami, too, failed to influence her, and wisely she gave up interfering in Yashodhara's way of life. She thought it would be best for her to leave Yashodhara free to follow her own course of life.

When time was thus sprawling, and stretching at a passive pace, a sudden bolt from the blue jolted Yashodhara and all the people in Kapilavastu.

Siddhartha Gautama attained enlightenment. Now he was Gautama Buddha. No, not even that. He was just the Buddha, the one who attained enlightenment under the Bodhi tree.

The long-awaited news reached Yashodhara.

Her life's ambition was achieved. Her passionate longing was peacefully subdued.

Kusala perceived divine peace, knowledge and understanding emanating from the tranquil countenance of Yashodhara.

She felt that she was blessed.

That day, Yashodhara explained to Kusala how Siddhartha yearned to attain true knowledge of the world; how he yearned to set humanity free from all kinds of sorrow. She told her that such a noble person as Siddhartha who sacrificed his personal life for the deliverance of humankind could never be owned by individuals or by families or even kingdoms as their own. Kusala was once again astonished by the ease with which Yashodhara disowned Siddhartha.

Now, Kapilavastu regularly received news of the Buddha's achievements. They heard how mighty kings gave up their dreadful weapons to take up the shields of peace and non-violence to protect their fellow human beings from poverty, hunger, diseases and natural calamities. They heard how great scholars and staunch supporters of other faiths were humbled by the supreme knowledge and wisdom of the

Buddha. They heard how the rich and the poor alike were casting off their prejudices of caste and creed and joining the Buddhist sangha to turn the whole world into a single, universal family.

Now, Kapilavastu was awaiting the arrival of the Buddha. People wanted to see him, listen to him and walk on the path of true knowledge. Yashodhara was never affected by such news. She continued to be silent, meditating by herself.

At last Kapilavastu received the news that its people had been waiting for. The Buddha was arriving.

People were delighted. Suddhodana and Gotami were overjoyed.

Yashodhara remained silent, lonely and peaceful.

Kusala could not contain her curiosity. She wanted to know how Yashodhara was feeling in her heart, and she questioned her about it.

Yashodhara answered in a calm and dispassionate tone.

'The Buddha is not an individual human being. The Buddha is the righteous path of living. I, too, am on the same path. I, too, am not an individual human being but one set on the course of righteous living. Hence I need not go to visit Gautama Buddha.'

'Tomorrow, when he arrives, Rahul will get the opportunity to see the person who he thinks is his father. Suddhodana and Gotami will get the opportunity to see the one who they think is their son. But I have no relationship left to establish my identity with him. Long ago, I freed myself from all such bonds.'

Kusala could imbibe the truth slowly.

Siddhartha was Gautama Buddha, and Yashodhara was Yasho Buddha. The Buddha arrived and then left.

Rahul saw his father and then followed the Buddha to receive his inheritance. Ananda saw his stepbrother and then followed the Buddha to join the sangha. A few years later, Suddhodana passed away peacefully.

Gotami felt lonely. There was no one with whom she could share her sorrow. Yashodhara was there in the house, but her existence was of little consolation to Gotami as she remained a dispassionate spectator of the events taking place in the household.

Gotami was deeply agitated. She failed to understand whether her present life had any meaning.

At first she believed that the purpose of her life was to bring up Siddhartha as his mother. But Siddhartha had long abandoned her.

Then, she believed that her life was meant to bring up Rahul, the son of Siddhartha. But eventually, not only Rahul but also her own son Ananda abandoned her under the influence of the Buddha.

After that, she felt she must live to look after her life partner, Suddhodana, who was growing old and weak.

But now he too had left her side, leaving her completely lonely.

'Why did my life become so miserable and meaningless?' she questioned herself. 'Who is to be blamed for all that has happened? Is it because of Siddhartha or, perhaps, because of Yashodhara?'

Yashodhara had been waiting for an opportunity when she would be able to make her mother-in-law realize the real purpose of human life.

One day she went to see Gotami. She sat in front of her and addressed her.

'I can understand your agony, Mother,' she said placidly. 'When you have a sumptuous dinner before you, will it not be foolish on your part to suffer from hunger? The Buddha has undertaken the noble task of offering relief from misery. But strangely, no woman has approached him to seek relief from sorrow and achieve eternal peace.'

'I do not know whether the Buddha will allow women to join the sangha. But you can go and try. If you join the sangha, you will be freed from sorrow. Your mind is tormented by unpleasant questions related to existence. Such torment is the outcome when we build relationships with others and when they fail to support us. Till now you have been trying to look at the Buddha as your son. You must give up that attitude. Such an attitude will do you no good, and it will not be helpful to him either. Think of him as a noble teacher who can set you free from ignorance. Then everything will change for you. You must achieve freedom; freedom from the bonds that make you miserable. Then, you will be left with only one bond – the bond called service to humanity. And that bond will never make you miserable.'

Gotami stared at Yashodhara for a while. She nodded her head and sighed in relief.

She left the house in quest of the Buddha dharma.

When Yashodhara received the news that the Buddha had permitted Gotami to join the sangha, she said to Kusala: 'Women, after all, are human beings. They, too, are eligible to receive the supreme knowledge and attain deliverance. I knew the Buddha would open the way for women.'

Kusala could see, hear and feel the bliss with which she spoke those words.

'From now onwards, nurturing familial relationships will not be a compelling bond to which women should bind their lives. Even if they bind themselves with such chains, they are now free to unchain themselves whenever they feel like doing it. Come, let us step into the wide, open world. Let us teach people how they can free themselves from sorrow. Let us experience the bliss which we get through serving humanity. Let us be a part of the crowd and search for our individual identity from within the group. Let us maintain constant communion with the crowd by being silent and alone. Let us experience the value of loneliness and silence by being one with the crowd.'

Kusala joined her palms to show her respect to Yashodhara. She was filled with gratitude for Yasho Buddha, who had delivered her from ignorance and showed her the true path of knowledge.

The two of them went to a nearby Buddhist sangha and took a vow to dedicate their lives to the Buddhist dharma.

Whenever Kusala tried to recall those valuable moments, they came back to her mind with such liveliness, she felt she was experiencing them all over again.

Yashodhara did not confine herself to meditation and preaching of the Buddhist dharma.

She loved to attend to the sick.

She studied which medicines become useful in treating different kinds of diseases. She discovered that words of kindness and affection were more helpful than medicines in treating the sick. She attended to her work with great dedication and felt satisfied only when the sick recovered from their illness. Everyone who knew her felt that the real purpose and meaning of her life was to relieve the sick of their suffering.

Kusala moved with Yashodhara and helped her in all her accomplishments as a Buddhist female monk. For that reason, the thought that Yashodhara ceased to be alive refused to enter her mind. She was being carried away by the flood of thoughts associated with Yasho Buddha when the voices of the monks, calling her from outside the room, reached her ears and pulled her out of the stream.

She was the only person who knew how Yashodhara had become the Buddha, and it was her responsibility to convey the news to those who should know.

Thinking about her responsibility, she left the room and declared that Yasho Buddha had attained parinirvana.

www.ingramcontent.com/pod-product-compliance
Ingram Content Group UK Ltd.
Pitfield, Milton Keynes, MK11 3LW, UK
UKHW042000230426
12048UKWH00009B/448